LIFE IN MEASURES

An Ink. Writing Group Anthology

Copyright © 2019 by Ink. Writing Group

All rights reserved. This book or any portion thereof may not be reproduced or used in any manner whatsoever without the express written permission of the publisher except for the use of brief quotations in a book review.

Printed in the United States of America

First Printing, 2019

ISBN 9781701150140

Amazon KDP Publishing

Cover design by Lindsey Sanford

LIFE IN MEASURES

We would like to apologize in advance to our readers for any earworms this anthology creates.

The short stories in this anthology were all inspired by a song of the writer's choosing.

Pendant Qu'ils Dorment, Un Beau Cadavre by Anthony Alaniz (*adult content warning*)
"Plus Putes que toutes les Putes" by ORTIS 1

Killer Queen by Josh Berry
"Killer Queen" by Queen 18

Marry Me by Ashley Gilsdorf
"Marry Me" by Thomas Rhett 30

Once in a Blue Moon: A Kip and Peggies Adventure by Charlee Kressbach
"Blue Moon" by Lorenz Hart and Richard Rogers 43

Good Vibrations by David McFarland
"Good Vibrations" by The Beach Boys 53

Blind Love by Katey Morgan (*adult content warning*)
"I Only Have Eyes for You" by The Flamingos 67

Song of the Dragonborn by Corinth Panther
"Song of the Dragonborn" by Jeremy Soule (from SKYRIM) 84

Ghosts by Alexis Parlier

"Green" by Ben Rector 93

The Song the Summer Sang by Lindsey Sanford

"You're Still You" by Josh Groban 112

Take Me Home by Kirsten Stiver

"How Great Thou Art" by Carl Boberg 132

Meet the author

Pendant Qu'ils Dorment, Un Beau Cadavre

By Anthony Alaniz

Ethan waited on the curb, hands buried deep in his pockets, shoulders hunched to fend off a light breeze that squeezed its way between the docile apartment buildings lining the street. They were modest dwellings, reaching half a dozen stories into the night sky. But Ethan didn't spend much time looking at them, instead keeping his chin buried in his chest. Eyes down. Waiting.

A young couple emerged from the shadows down the street. Their bodies entwined, pulsating. A maudlin murmuration. Ethan glanced. They wafted down the deserted street toward Ethan and the *Le Syndicat de Paris* behind him. As they neared, tipping and tilting, reeling as their world spun, giggles punctuated slurred French. They wandered around Ethan, avoiding proximity out of some drunken French dignity, before pushing their way through the door of the bar. Heavy bass spilled into the groggy street. The door closed, and quiet returned.

Ethan felt his phone buzz in his pants pocket. He ignored it.

Come on, man, Ethan thought.

An engine revved, accelerating, growing closer. Louder. The engine reverberated down the narrow street, ricocheting off the apartments. A light bobbed and weaved, navigating the curve to the north. A pair of headlights appeared from the same direction as the young couple. A black SUV. Something German and luxurious. It stopped in front of him.

Ethan sprang from the curb, walking around the SUV. The rear door opened and a man stepped out.

"Damnit, Cameron, where the hell have you been?" Ethan bombarded Cameron — standing six inches taller helped.

"It's taken care of," Cameron said, closing the car door and weaseling past Ethan who followed him around the back of the SUV.

"What does that mean? Are you sure? She—"

Cameron turned. The SUV sped off leaving the two in the middle of the street.

"She won't be a problem."

"I didn't—"

"You didn't do anything," Cameron said. "You were both drunk." He smiled.

"No. I wasn't. And you know that."

"But she doesn't know that. And you won't tell her."

Ethan paused, his shoulders loosening.

"So it's done?"

"It's done...now let's have some fun before we leave. I have the lawyer on retainer through Monday."

The two walked into *Le Syndicat de Paris*.

* * *

Ethan stood at the urinal, dick in his hand, leaning his head against the wall, uncertain if he was finished. The bathroom door opened with a bang and the shuffling of inebriated legs. Laughter, high-pitched, pierced the tiny tiled bathroom. Not even the heavy thump from the dance floor could drown out her giggles.

A woman.

Ethan straightened, pulling himself upright off the wall under his own horny power. He tried to get a look at them, but they quickly slipped into the lone stall. The *tink* of various clasps, snaps, buttons, and zippers relieved of duty echoed. A deep grunt and a soft moan washed over the stall wall.

Damn.

Certain enough he was finished, he slipped himself back into his pants, zipped, and walked out.

* * *

A white horn adorned with a tiny tin cup slid into view. A pale mixture stared back. Ice shifted and stirred. Ethan lifted his head, focusing his eyes on the bartender.

"What's this?" Ethan asked, gesturing at the drink with one hand while gripping the bar counter with the other.

The bartender looked right and pointed to the other end of the bar. Ethan turned, and a woman in red stared back. He tilted his head, raising an eyebrow at her, trying to focus. She lifted her drink and smiled. Ethan turned back to the bartender who chuckled.

"Be careful, son," he said in accented English with a broad smile carved into his face.

Ethan looked back down the bar, looking for his lady in red, but she was gone. Ethan craned his neck, trying to spot her bright red dress in the sea of revelers. He turned, hoping to keep his spot at the bar while he –- A hand traced across his lower back. He whirled around, meeting her bright blue eyes with his.

"Oh, hi," Ethan said.

"Oh, hi," she smiled.

"Thank you for the drink."

"You like it?"

"Haven't tried it."

"It's a house special."

"I don't want to get drunk. Not anymore."

"Oh, why's that?" She leaned in, looking up at him with just her eyes. "You don't want to make any..." She grabbed his tie. "...bad..." She pulled him closer, his lips closer. "...decisions?" Their lips touched. She pressed into him.

He kissed her, then pulled back.

"No. I love making bad decisions." He leaned away, slouching on the bar –- a bad Han Solo. "It's just..." He trailed off.

"What is it?"

"Well, I'd like to remember the bad decisions we make tonight."

She smiled, sipping her drink. "Ooooh, clever boy."

* * *

"Where you from?" he yelled, unconvinced she could hear him over the blaring music. The crowd swirled around them. The bartender flocked back and forth tending drink orders. People danced.

"Not going to ask my name first?" She sipped the drink clasped between her hands. "Interesting move."

"Ha...yeah. I'm Ethan. From Boston. Born and raised in Iowa though."

"Sounds...exotic."

"It's, uh, not." He sipped his drink, tipping the pointed horn upward. The ice shifted, drink dribbling out the side of his mouth, trickling down his chin.

The lady in red leaned in quickly, licking from his chin to his lips, kissing him.

"Delicious," she said.

"Yeah. It's good."

"I'm Alessia. Alessia Solzi."

"Oh, are you French? I don't hear an--"

"No ... no. Not French. I'm ... Parisian. Lived here all my life though."

Ethan smiled. "Interesting. Why the distinction?"

Alessia glanced at him. "Reasons," she said.

Ethan leaned back, raising his hands in a half surrender. "That's fair."

Fair echoed through the bar as the song faded to nothing — a first for the night. The crowd swished and swayed as exhausted dancers jostled to the bar for refueling. The building was narrow but deep. The bar sat to the right when you walked in from the street. To the left was a single row of plush chairs and tiny tables best for fancy fruity drinks and appetizers. At the back there was just enough room for a DJ and small dance floor before another lounge area and the restrooms tucked in the back. Another door at the back led to a small kitchen tucked behind the bathrooms.

"I think the next song is mine," Alessia gleamed.

"What is it?"

"Do you know French?"

"No," Ethan said, flushed. "I know enough to get me into trouble, but not enough to get myself out of it." *Woo, that was a stiff drink.*

"Cute."

Ethan leaned into Alessia, slipping his arm around her waist. She leaned into him, putting her head on his shoulder. Ethan watched Alessia in the mirror behind the bar, eyes closed, smiling.

A synth-pop wave grew from the back and receded. Grew and receded. It grew a third time, accompanied by a pelting beat that filled the bar, overpowering the synth-pop wave. The percussion entered, commanding order, building before the drop.

Alessia shrieked. "I love this song so much!"

"What's it about?"

"Bad things."

"Fun bad things?"

"Perhaps for one of us." She winked.

"Oh, why not both?"

"I don't know your kinks."

"Kinks?"

"Mhmm." She sipped her drink.

Has she gotten another? She's nursing it.

Ethan pulled out his phone to check the time — past midnight. A lone text message from Cameron was the only notification. It wasn't even a text, just the lone image of him, naked, standing behind a woman who was naked as well, holding the phone. His hands covered her breasts, and nothing else. Her head rested on his shoulder, her eyes closed, mouth agape. A red dress sat crumpled on the floor behind them.

When did he leave? Ethan couldn't remember; probably ducked out without a goodbye.

"Everything okay?"

"Yeah. Just lost a friend. He left already."

"Was he your ride?"

"No. I was gonna Uber back to the hotel."

"Where's that?"

"Back on the right bank in the 9th Arrindis..."

"*Arrondissement*..... That's too far." She paused. "How about we get out of here? Go back to my place?" Her eyes grew wide. "It's just down the street. We can walk."

"Yeah. Okay. Let's go"

* * *

Alessia stood outside on the curb. Waiting. Glancing back, she saw Ethan leaning over the bar deep in conversation with the bartender. Ethan reached inside his coat, pulling out his wallet, but the bartender shook his head, pointing outside at Alessia. Ethan turned to her, then turned back to the bartender who chuckled.

Ethan pushed away from the bar and wiggled his way through the crowd to the door. The bartender met Alessia's eyes and nodded. She returned a smile. The heavy bass again tumbled into the street like a college drunk. But just as quickly as the sound erupted into the night did it disappear as the door closed.

"You paid my tab?"

"Of course. It's the least I could do."

"You didn't have to. But thanks."

"You owe me, though."

"Do I?"

"One kiss. No peck though. A passionate one."

"I think I can do that."

Ethan leaned in, the two in the middle of the deserted street outside the bar, and they kissed. Her arms wrapped around him, her nails scratching down his back, sending chills scurrying across his neck. Their mouths contorted, teasing each other. Slowly, she pulled away, smiling, her face flush.

"Which way?"

"This way." Alessia twirled Ethan, leading him, her hand wrapped in his.

***

"What do you do?" Ethan asked.

They'd been walking for a while, but Ethan had lost track of time. Few shops were open, and those that were open could have closed hours ago. No one was out. The black storefronts and boutique shop fronts blurred into dazzling reflections of a quiet city.

"A little of this, a little of that," Alessia said, her fingers intertwined with his. "I stay busy."

"Oooh, mysterious." Ethan chuckled. "Would you have to kill me if you told me?"

"Maybe."

Her pace quickened, pulling Ethan around a sweeping corner. She came to a sudden stop in front of a small, green building that looked like an oversized Catholic confessional booth. A haphazard set of green walls awkwardly connected it to the building next door.

Alessia pulled him into her, her face turned up toward his, pressing her lips into his. Ethan wrapped his arms around her, his hands wandering. She snaked her arm between them, slipping her hand in his pants, feeling him get hard.

He moaned, kissing her, when suddenly she pulled back.

"I have an idea!" She turned toward the green building.

"Where are we?" Ethan asked, trying to read the tall, white sign plastered to the left of the entryway, desperate to find the English translation.

"The Catacombs."

"The what?" He glanced at her.

"*Catacombes de paris...entrée....* It's the entrance to the Paris Catacombs."

"Cool?" Ethan looked around.

"Let's go inside."

"Now? Isn't it closed?"

Alessia walked to the mesh door and opened it, revealing a black hole.

"Follow me." Alessia walked into the darkness. The door hung open.

"Alessia?" He whispered.

Nothing.

"Alessia?"

A light flickered inside, illuminating a small anteroom. Alessia wasn't there.

"Come on, silly, it's safe. Follow me."

Ethan crept into the building, his eyes slowly adjusting to the bright fluorescents. The small room was the top of downward spiraling stairs. He could hear Alessia shuffling below.

"Hey!" Ethan called. "Coming." He slowly descended, leaning against the white stone as he held onto the rail. *Not a good time to be drunk*, he thought.

* * *

"Alessia? Where are you?" Ethan reached the bottom of the stairs. He was in another small room, this one filled with large placards chronicling the catacombs' history. An opening along the wall led into the catacombs.

He listened for Alessia to respond, but he heard nothing. Ethan looked around, moving from placard to placard—6 MILLION BURIED HERE read one, sending a chill crashing over him. PASSAGES REMAIN HIDDEN read another.

Ethan heard shuffling from the corridor. Alessia poked her head around the corner.

"You coming?"

"Why are we here?"

"We're going to my place, remember?"

Ethan looked at her. He felt his face contort in confusion.

"You don't..." Ethan started.

"No, silly. It's a shortcut. It's cool. Come on."

Ethan hesitated. *You've been in dumber situations*, he thought.

"What you waiting for?" she said. Her eyes looked him over. "Maybe this will persuade you?"

She reached out, pulling him by his waistband. She grabbed his hand, guiding it down her thigh to the hem of her dress, sliding his hand back up her leg. She wrapped his fingers around the top of her panties and pulled, sliding them down her legs. She lifted one foot, then the other, slipping them off.

"That was hot," Ethan said.

"Mmhmm. Follow me."

Alessia headed into the Catacombs. Dark brown bones, cast in pale yellow light, lined the walls. Nameless skulls with empty eyes followed the two as they headed beneath Paris.

*　*　*

Alessia stopped at a dead end. Bones, not as brown with age as the others, stared back.

"Dead end," Ethan said.

Alessia said nothing, letting go of his hand and walking up to the wall. Her hands traced over the bones, touching each one she passed. Her hand paused over one near the center of the wall and pushed. A loud *click* shook the walls. There was a deep click somewhere in the ceiling, and the wall swung away, revealing a hidden passage.

Alessia walked over the threshold.

"This way," she said. Ethan followed.

"These hidden passages are scattered underneath Paris." She walked near the wall, her hand running over the old bones. "Six million people are said to be buried…" She trailed off.

"Yeah…read that."

"It's beautiful."

The corridor twisted this way and that. Sharp turns punctuated lazy curves deep underneath Paris. Ethan had no idea where they were. Or how to get back. Or where they were going. They walked in silence, Alessia drifting from one corridor wall to another. The deeper they went, the colder the air got, chilling Ethan. The dampness didn't help either. The stale air tickled his nose. It smelled rotten.

"How much further?"

"Almost there."

Up ahead was another sharp turn. Alessia scurried, disappearing, leaving Ethan behind.

"Hurry," she whispered. He lumbered forward.

Ethan turned the corner to find another dead end. Alessia stood against the wall, naked, her red dress in a pile in the corner. A small mattress covered in a thin sheet sat at her feet. Lit candles hugged the walls even though a bright fluorescent light hung overhead. Everything gleamed white. Ethan stood stunned.

"Uh…"

"What?" Alessia said, pressing herself against the skull-lined wall. "Is this weird?" She vaguely gestured

"A little." Ethan began undoing his belt. She licked the wall.

"I'm sorry. I thought you were the type of guy…" She watched as he unbuttoned his pants, untucked his shirt, and unzipped his pants. He loosened his tie, unbuttoned his shirt. His pants slipped low on his hips. He kicked off one shoe, then another, his pants falling around his ankles.

Alessia's eyes slowly scanned down his body.

"Already excited?"

"A little."

"That's not little." Her eyes darted down to his crotch. "Lie down."

Ethan stepped out of his pants, peeling his shirt off, tossing it on the ground. He climbed onto the mattress. Alessia stood over him straddling him, looking down at him.

"You're gorgeous," Ethan said, running his hands up her thighs.

"Thank you." Alessia slowly lowered herself. Her fingers wrapped around his cock, guiding him into her. His hips arched. She moaned. "It feels so good."

He ran his hands up her body, cupping her breasts. He tried to sit up to kiss her, but Alessia pushed him back, holding him down.

"Not yet," she said.

Alessia sat there, eyes closed, hips static. Ethan tried to move his hips in hopes of igniting something, but Alessia didn't move.

"Uhh..." he said.

"Just wait," she whispered. Ethan turned his head, staring at the skulls that were staring back.

This is creepy, he thought. *But she's so...*

That's when Ethan noticed the skulls staring back weren't the dark brown, mildewed skulls from centuries ago. These were white—pristine. Fresh. His eyes darted across the wall. They were all white—new—except one. It wasn't brown—discolored from centuries of underground living. A reddish spray pattern covered it. Ethan reached out, running his hand over the skull. It felt wet. He pulled his hand back and looked at it. They were stained red.

He whipped his head back to Alessia who was watching him, but she was different. Black eyes stared back. There was no distinction between pupil, iris, and the whites of her eyes. Her piercing blue hue was gone.

"What the fuck!" Ethan tried to struggle, twisting beneath her, but he couldn't move. She was too heavy. Too strong. He was weak. Drunk.

He began hitting her, punching her. His fist caught her in the jaw, knocking her head back, but her body didn't budge. She slowly turned back to him.

"Who are you?!" Ethan screamed.

"We have a mutual friend," Alessia said. A thin trail of blood dribbled from the corner of her mouth. She leaned over him, her face inches from his. Ethan gagged as she breathed, coughing. Her hand slipped under the mattress. A clink of metal on stone froze Ethan. Her hand emerged holding a long knife with a curved blade. The ornate handle glistened. It looked old.

"Who?" Ethan asked.

"Oh, you know who she is, Ethan. Remember, you weren't drunk. And how could you forget her, Ethan? The way you pulled down her pants while she was passed out on the couch. You had to undress her just to spread her legs far enough to fit inside her. But that didn't stop you from huffing and puffing your way to orgasm. It took you, what, a minute? Two to finish? Pathetic."

"I don't know what you're..."

"Don't lie, Ethan. Lying won't help you now. She had lacerations, Ethan, inside her. She still bleeds."

"I'm sorry. I didn't mean to. I..."

Alessia's hand flashed across his neck, filleting it open. His hands flew to his throat as blood shot into the air, spritzing the white skulls that watched. Blood seeped through his fingers, pooling on the mattress beneath him. There was no pain, just warmth.

Footsteps echoed through the corridor, growing louder. Ethan tried to scream, but only a gurgle stumbled out, barely audible. His breathing labored. A pain crept in his chest as his lungs filled with blood. His eyes wide, he tried to see who was coming.

A slender figure turned the corner. The shadow held something large in her hand. A woman materialized in the same red dress Alessia wore. In her hand was a decapitated head.

"About time," Alessia said.

"He was fun," said the second woman in red. "How could I not?" She leaned over Ethan, sticking a finger into the pool of blood beneath his head. She licked it before putting it in Alessia's mouth.

"He tastes so good," Alessia said as she pulled the woman in red toward her, kissing her.

Ethan coughed, blood spurting from his mouth. His hands fell away from his neck as blood continued to burble from the slice. Alessia slowly lifted herself off him.

"Oh...he has angel lust." She flicked the tip of his still erect penis. "Cute."

Alessia picked up her dress.

"Leave the head. It'll be awhile before he bleeds out."

"Yes, my queen."

The new woman in red placed the head on Ethan's chest. Cameron's eyes stared back.

"Good night, Ethan," Alessia said, taking the woman's hand in hers. They walked off, turning the corner.

Ethan listened as the footsteps faded away. Silence enveloped him as he fought to keep his eyes open. A shiver rocked his body. Deep in the Catacombs he heard the familiar loud click that shook the walls when the secret passage opened. Ethan struggled to move. To scream. To save his life. The hall shook with a thud as the passage closed and everything fell silent.

Tears cascaded down his cheeks.

The corridor went dark.

Killer Queen

By Josh Berry

Doctor Sung laughed maniacally as he sat behind the control booth, awaiting the imminent death of his arch nemesis, Joan Jewett.

"So," he said, "you thought you could intercept my evil plan to collude with the United States by tampering with their food supply. You fool!"

Joan was unable to defend herself. Her weapons were taken away from her, and she was laid on a slab of cement barred down with metal chains preventing her from moving.

"Doctor," she replied, "you are mad! If this plan is successful, all American men will lose their sex drive and the country will cease to be populated."

"That's the point," he said. "Try getting out of this one, Joan."

With that, he turned a mysterious dial. *Shwoop shwoop shwoop shwoop.* Joan feared the worst. To her left, amidst the numerous vials and beakers in the dark, concrete lab, a chamber opened up in the cement walls. Slowly emerging from the chamber was a thick laser beam coming towards her chest, waiting to slice her in half and end her life.

As afraid as she was in this situation, she still managed to detach herself from the situation and form a plan.

Aha, she thought, *the elemental double bond separator!*

Joan squirmed to reach the separator from the pocket of her mother's navy blue corduroy trench coat she was currently wearing. The beam was inches from her chest, and in the moment she gathered all her strength and grabbed it. The metal bars fastening her down were destroyed.

The enemy saw her and fired at her. She then took whatever vials and beakers were lying around and threw them on the ground, creating a cloud of smoke around her. Taking advantage of the situation, she gathered her weapons and attempted to leave.

It appeared to be an easy escape, until out of the blue Dr. Sung jumped onto her like a leaping panther in the wilderness.

"As long as I am here you will not escape alive."

She abruptly bent forward and flipped him on his back. Immediately afterwards she clicked her heels together, revealing blades between the heels and shoes which she stuck up to Dr. Sung's neck.

"Escape alive, huh? Not in my neck of the woods."

She then slit his throat with her shoes, clicked her heels again to conceal the blades, and left as silently as a light breeze on a tepid spring day.

* * *

Joan soon returned to her apartment in Yingtan to sell it. Due to her career, she was never a person known to live in one place for very long, in order to avoid complications with any foreign governments. The day after, she took what was important and boarded a plane to Tokyo. This was not her desired destination, though, as she was strategic enough not to live too close to major cities, but rather smaller towns relatively nearby so as to avoid being found in the most obvious of places. Because of this, she was instead stationed at the coast-side town of Choshi. Thanks to her affiliation with the U.S. government, and her handy-dandy working visa, she was able to find a place of residence quicker than the average legal migrant.

As she settled down in her futon to partake in a good night's sleep for once, she opened her beloved locket. In it was the last picture taken of her with her mother before she was deployed to her final mission in Shanghai. She had died at the hands of Dr. Sung when Joan was only four years old.

"I did it mother," she said. "I avenged you. May you now rest peacefully..."

Joan then kissed the locket and prepared for sleep.

...and may I find a new purpose.

Joan had a sleep of restlessness. The violence she had been forced by the CIA to partake in ,was not what she wanted. It was never what she wanted. Her mind hearkened back to her days as a child. More specifically, the worst day she ever endured in her living days.

"No, don't," she cried as she was held at gunpoint by the then up-and-coming crime boss, Dr. Chiao Sung.

"Now we will see who you love more little one. Is it your mother or is it you? You have five minutes to decide."

Joan's mother reached out her hand from her cell and clung to her daughter's hand tightly to say her final goodbyes.

"Be strong now," she said. "This man's not going to separate us."

"Really?" Joan said wiping what she had decided would be the final tears she would cry.

"Yes, not if I have anything to say about it. I won't be gone forever. It'll only be a little bit. Remember that time daddy and I went on a trip to Mexico?"

"Yeah, and you left me at Grandpa's house?"

"Yes, I'm just going to Mexico again."

"But you're not coming back."

"That's true, but that doesn't mean we won't see each other soon."

Dirtied by her previous beatings during incarceration, Joan clung warmly to her mother's strong, loving arms. Joan had decided on her mother's life, because she trusted her mother's judgment far more than her own.

Joan, in her present form, was awakened by the visions her demons prepared before her. Within the shadows of the night, they performed a marionette show of tormenting memories never to be erased regardless of a desire to do so like a vanishing mist in the air.

Joan's phone rang. It was the general.

"I take it you've established yourself in Tokyo, is that correct?"

"Yeah," she replied. "I moved in about two hours away from there. Can't come off as too conspicuous, now can I?"

"I guess old habits die hard."

"Alright, what's happening now? Why did you call me and send me to Tokyo? Is it to congratulate me or is my mission not over yet?"

"It appears we haven't dissolved Sung's crime ring just yet. There's still one more inside man you missed."

"What's his name?"

"Uhhh..."

"C'mon now, spit it out. You expect me to do my job, don't you?"

"Nikolaus Chekhov."

"Wait a minute, you mean that D&D dweeb I dated in college?"

"Yep, it's the same one. Judging from the information you intercepted for us last time, it appears he was an ambassador for Sung's ring. He persuaded powerful leaders to collude with the crime ring under the guise that they would not cause harm to humanity."

"I got that, but what if he catches me? My cover will be blown and then I'll never get to him."

"Don't you remember the briefing from our last mission? Everytime Sung hired someone, he'd use his memory erasing device to brainwash his employees."

"I take it no-nip Nik will be no different."

"Yes, and pardon me for asking but 'no-nip Nik'?"

"It's a long story, but for time's sake, some broad dated him for a short time and then this rumor spread around that he had no nipples. Once that cat was let out of the bag, every girl started dating him for curiosity's sake."

"Aha, that is quite humorous. Anyway, we have agents surrounding the area to ensure your safety. All you have to do is work your seductive magic, get in his room, kill him quickly, and leave without anyone knowing."

"Ah, but you know me. I never leave without anyone knowing. I'd much prefer to make a spectacle of things."

"As long as you don't get caught, then do as you please. Your mission begins tomorrow. Don't let us down. Goodnight, miss."

"Goodnight."

* * *

The following night, Joan took the public transport to Tokyo. She checked her watch.

22:46, she thought, *right on time.*

She arrived at a local underground club in a seedier part of town. The neon was burnt out on many of the stores and restaurants, and pedestrians were scarce. She was told by her instructor that the club was called the "Kancho," but due to her inability to read Japanese, she ended up guessing which destination was her desired one. Loud beats were emerging from a grimy, dank alleyway.

This has to be it, she thought.

She crept in through the dank, ratty alleyway that looked like all the places her parents told her not to go near combined into one. She entered the club and went downstairs where the action was happening. Lights were flashing, people were necking and feeling each other up, and the beats were even louder than when Joan was outside.

These people are probably on all sorts of illicit substances. she thought. *I'll let the local police handle that. Right now I gotta find my guy.*

Joan found it typical for the men she'd often seduce to be off to the side at the mini-bar. This was so as not to draw attention to themselves as they were usually wanted federal criminals. This time was no exception, as Nikolaus was sitting half-drunk talking to the bartender (or yelling rather, due to the volume of the music).

"Hey," Joan said approaching Nikolaus. "What are you doing here?"

"Get out," he replied. "I need time to think."

"Well you certainly won't be able to think when you're in a loud place like this."

"You're right"

"You got a place around here to call home?"

"A hotel room actually, but I don't need to get entangled with any woman at the moment. I got laid off. I need some time to think."

"If you needed to think so badly, why'd you come here? There's plenty of bars all around this city."

"They speak English here."

"Well if you're so resistant to speaking Japanese, you couldn't have picked a worse country to visit. Here, I'll take you home."

"No thank you."

"Well, it seems you don't have any other friends down here that are sober and will understand you, so I might as well. It's the least I can do."

"Okay."

"Believe me, as far as women go I'm one of the last people you have to worry about getting 'entangled with.'"

The two then continued to talk for a good forty-five minutes until Nikolaus became so inebriated he had no choice but to let Joan take him back to his hotel room.

* * *

In Nikolaus's hotel room, Joan fawned herself all over Nikolaus. She kissed up and down his neck in a moment of pure, calculated passion. Nikolaus rubbed her back as she disrobed into the slip she wore underneath. She rubbed his arms and kissed his forehead like the true love machine she was trained to be. It was then that the moment of truth came. She unbuttoned his shirt, and lo and behold, the rumors were true.

No nipples, she thought. *If only I hadn't devoted my life to spy work, I'd try and reach out to my college girls in a heartbeat. This is too good to be true.*

* * *

Once the intimacy ended, and the clock had silently struck 3:00 A.M. Joan snuck out of bed and into Nikolaus's bathroom. In her purse she carried a bomb she had made the previous day. There were creaky floorboards in this particular traditional Japanese hotel, so now she was faced with the challenge of not only not being caught by Nikolaus, but not being heard by him either. Then there was the escape plan. How was she to escape this room? It was a second story room, so she had to exit quietly and make sure nobody in neighboring rooms knew she had left the room.

She tippy-toed out of the bathroom and made sure no boards were heard. Not a single quiet tap was heard from her feet simply coming in contact with the floor. Finally she placed the bomb underneath his bed. *Click click.* It was activated. She then peered up and noticed a window in the room. She looked out it.

Aha, she thought, *an onsen bath! If I get caught I can just jump into there!*

Just then a light came on. Nikolaus pulled out a gun.

"What are you doing?" he asked.

She walked slowly to the main door to leave. Nikolaus gripped the gun harder and put his finger on the trigger in preparation.

Then, in an unexpected move, Joan ran towards the window and broke through it, jumping into the nearby hot springs. She swam like the wind as Nikolaus fired five rounds at her. Only one of the rounds hit her in the hand. She then leapt over the fence and ran the streets of Tokyo until she was clear out of Nikolaus's sight. She was not out of range of sound, though, as she could still hear him yelling at her.

"What did you do?" he yelled, "What did you do to my room you filthy—"

The hotel room blew up, and Nikolaus was no more.

* * *

The following morning, Joan returned to her rented apartment in Choshi to report back with headquarters.

"...And the other people in the hotel survived?"

"..."

"They survived right?"

"It appears that at least six other casualties were caused. Don't worry, there was no one who saw you and local police appear to be blaming it on a nearby serial killer named Kira. At this rate, there's absolutely no way you'll be held accountable."

"I've killed many severe threats to the United States, and that was all fine by me, but to take the life of somebody by accident is something I can't live with."

"You won't have to. We're moving you to France next week. There's been reporting of a terrorist group hiding in Cannes."

"No you won't. Goodbye General."

Joan closed the laptop.

I can't believe it, she thought to herself, *using me like that. My original agreement was to eliminate every member of Sung's crime ring, and then they go and use me like the agreement meant nothing.*

She then got up and took her laptop to a nearby pier. With all her force, she threw the laptop into the harbor.

"Sayonara, CIA," she said.

As she tried walking back, she noticed something. It was her locket. She opened it and looked deeply at it. This time, when she looked at it, it almost appeared as if her mother was clapping for her and smiling a happier smile than ever before. Through the tears, Joan held her fist in the air like a tired, wounded, soldier coming out victorious.

"I did it mother. I did what you couldn't finish. I know you're proud of me, I just know it."

She then took the locket and threw it in the sea also. Knowing all her work was done, she had no need for it anymore. She never wanted to be a spy, she never wanted to seduce men, she never wanted any of this, and neither did her mother before her. Her dreams were always centered on the hope of a normal life, a normal job, and a normal husband to cherish forever. As she tossed the locket into the water, a great burden had been relieved. The relief was so great that it took some time for it all to sink in.

She packed her things and headed for home in New Jersey. A new life awaited, a new dream awaited, a new person awaited. To her, the discarding of the locket was not to disrespect her mother's legacy but to honor it and to signal the beginning of a new chapter of her life.

"I'm here, Mom," she said to herself as she stepped off the plane. "I'm finally here."

Marry Me

By Ashley Gilsdorf

Saturday March 3, 2012

Drew kept pulling, attempting to win the mini game of tug-of-war that had commenced between him and his infuriating bow tie. If it had been up to him, he would have torn the offensive thing off, thrown it in the garbage, and pretended the tailor had forgotten to include it with his suit. But today wasn't about him. Today was about Allie. And for Allie, he would do anything.

"You need some help, son?" Allie's dad Fred asked as he came to look at the bow tie.

"Thanks Fred."

Seeing the proud look on Fred's face did little to dull the tense frustration Drew was feeling. Drew had to look around the room. Because no matter how close they were, Drew felt very uncomfortable looking Fred in the eye. So, he let his gaze wander out the den window next to him. His childhood backyard had been transformed. The trees and old tree house were surrounded by strings of light bulbs. There was a small white tent with beverages and hors d' oeuvres. A small arrangement of forty folding chairs was strategically placed into two groups of twenty to create an aisle out of the bit of freshly cut grass that was between them. There was a beautiful trellis that was framed by the magnolia trees. Drew smiled at the sight of them and couldn't help but think back to the day he first met Allie.

Saturday August 3, 2002

The unexpected heat beat down on Drew's back. It was early August and one of the hottest days on record in Sandusky, Ohio. Small beads of sweat were watering his brows. At thirteen, he didn't care much about the sun; he only cared about playing a game of baseball. The task was mighty tough to accomplish when you only had one brother and all the other kids in the neighborhood were scared of a little heat.

He and his brother both noticed the moving van pulling up the drive.

"Who moves in this type of weather?" his brother Kyle snarked.

"Who plays baseball in this type of weather?" Drew replied, mimicking his tone.

Kyle glared at Drew and then shouted, "Resume play!" throwing the baseball right at Drew's shoulder. At fourteen, Kyle was a pretty good ball player and the throw hurt like hell. Drew never let Kyle know he was hurt. So, Drew just gritted his teeth and brushed his shoulder as if a little bit of dirt had gotten on it.

They didn't really pay much attention to the new neighbors moving in. People moved in and out of their neighborhood all the time. It was nothing new to them, and they were far more interested in finishing their game. That was, until they reached the bottom of the ninth inning. Kyle tossed the ball over to Drew, but instead of hitting it forward, he popped a foul ball behind him and into the new neighbor's yard.

"Heads up!" Drew heard Kyle shout from his pitcher's spot

"No!" came a scream of protest from behind the hedge separating the two yards.

I injured someone. It was the only thought Drew had before he dropped his bat and he and his brother went sprinting around the hedge and over into the neighbor's yard.

"Is everyone alright?" he heard Kyle ask as he stood there dumbstruck by the pretty girl in front of him. She was a petite brunette about their age. She was wearing a pair of jean shorts and a tee shirt that said Gryffindor with the house crest on it. Even with her hands on her hips and a stern look on her face, Drew instantly knew he liked this girl. How could he not be in love with an evident Harry Potter fan?

"No, everyone is not okay. I am not okay."

"Where are you hurt?" Kyle asked.

"I am not hurt. One of you killed my magnolias." The girl's voice was thick with a Southern accent and she pointed to both him and his brother and back to the bush with broken branches. She looked at them both with a skeptical glare.

"Oh, I'm sorry," Drew said, finally finding his voice. "I hit the ball with the wrong part of the bat."

"I was looking forward to watching the magnolias bloom next spring. It was my favorite part of this new house and you ruined it."

"Is there anything I can do to help make it up to you?"

"You can get outta my yard and stay outta my way."

Saturday March 3, 2012
Drew thought she would never forgive him for killing her magnolias that first day. He saved up his allowance for a few months. Then, he bought them both tickets to go see the first screening of *Harry Potter and the Chamber of Secrets*. After that, she decided to give him a second chance and they quickly became inseparable.

"Gentlemen, gather for a toast." Frank waved everyone into the center of the room. "Well, I just wanted to say that I am so tickled. Today is the day when I give the love of my life, my daughter Allie, away. And that is pretty tough. I have to say it's a lot easier to do knowing that I am giving her to someone who loves my pumpkin just as much as I always have. Cheers to the happy couple!"

"Cheers," echoed a choir of voices.

Drew had to turn out and away from the group as he almost spat out the shot of whiskey he took from his engraved flask. His throat was so clogged with emotions, but he was determined not to let anyone see that he couldn't swallow the measly swig.

"You alright?" his brother Kyle asked with a raised brow.

"Something caught in my throat." Drew cleared his throat and tossed his flask back again, willing the liquid to slide down his throat with ease. Then, he set it down on the table in front of him.

"You'll be fine. No one will be looking at you anyway." Kyle clapped him on the back and then walked away to help the flower girl Sophie, who was asking an abundance of questions.

"How many magnolias should I throw as I go down the aisle? Do I need to pick up my dress so I don't step on it? What if I run out of flowers before I get up to the altar?"

The merry-go-round of questions made him dizzy just from hearing them. This wasn't doing him any favors in helping him to keep calm. Drew quickly scanned the room to find its occupants distracted by other tasks. So, he crept out the door nearest him.

On the other side, he found himself in the hallway of his old home. He started walking, just hoping that being away from the crush of people would help him with his battle for calm. He didn't have to walk far before he found his way into the kitchen. Drew looked around the space and once he was sure no one was around, let loose a muffled irritated groan. He kept trying to find the sense of peace with which he had started the day, but his attempts were being thwarted. And this room. This room reminded him of the first time he almost kissed her.

Friday, April 14, 2006
Drew glared at the burnt batch of cookies that he pulled out of his workstation in Home Economics class. It was moments like these when he seriously hated going to a liberal arts high school where classes like this were mandatory for everyone. He was a baseball player and planned to become an architect. Why in the world did

he need to know how to make a non-charred batch of cookies? Wasn't that the Keebler elf's job?

"Trying to burn down the oven so you don't fail?" Allie chuckled as she walked up to Drew's workstation and popped one of her perfectly baked cookies into her mouth with a satisfied grin.

"Ha, hilarious."

She grabbed an oven mitt and put it on as she swallowed the last of her cookie. Allie picked up one of the burnt blobs.

"Hey, look on the bright side. If you ever want to take up a new sport you have some free hockey pucks right here. Come on, even mandrake root couldn't save this petrified puck."

Drew just glared back at her and crossed his arms over his chest.

"Oh, lighten up. I can help with your technique. I will just come over to your house after school."

"Fine."

"And find a way to get fun Drew back when I come. Grumpy Drew is no fun."

"Fine," he grumbled again.

Later that evening, Allie came over to Drew's house to help him practice and perfect his baking skills. The kitchen was cluttered with baking gear: Mixing bowls, measuring cups, flour, rolling pins, and oven mitts. A couple of rejected batches of cookies were already in the nearby trash can.

"Woah, hold on! That's a tablespoon. The recipe calls for a teaspoon," Allie cautioned.

"Table, tea, what's the difference?"

Allie stared at him with a glare. "Come on. Please tell me you can see the difference." She pointed out the two different measuring spoons.

"Of course I can."

"Then you should realize mixing up the two would not be good for the recipe."

"Oh yeah? Well would this be good for my recipe?" He quickly grabbed a small bit of dry flour out of the mixing bowl in front of him and tossed it at her apron.

"Andrew Jacob Sanders, you did not just d--"

"Yes, I did." He picked up the bowl and flung another bit of flour into her hair.

"Oh, that is it." Allie grabbed the remaining bag of flour from the counter and began tossing it at Drew. The battle commenced and the kitchen quickly began to fill with flour. The whole area looked as if a mini sandstorm was passing through. A white cloud soon enveloped the whole space around them.

"Truce! Truce!" Allie set down the bag and held up her hands in the air.

"Truce." Drew set his bowl down on the counter.

The flour dust in the air quickly settled. The two looked at each other. They had flour everywhere. It was caked onto his tee-shirt. It was covering the surface of the face on her watch. It was caught behind his ears and making him twitch with an itchy feeling. It was stuck to the strands of her hair. The flour was on his eyebrows and it was invading the left corner of her mouth. Allie tried to blow the flour away, but it was caked to that spot. Before he could stop himself, his fingers had wiped away the spot. But then as if he had lost complete control over his motor functions, his fingers lingered on the spot. Drew felt his gaze being pulled to those lips which his fingers were lingering on. Then, he physically felt his upper body leaning into hers. He couldn't seem to stop himself from moving forward.

Until he heard the front door open. Then, he quickly stepped away from her. His brother walked in the door and his heart jumped up into his throat.

"What happened here?"

Drew's throat was as dry as a desert. He was relieved when he heard Allie say, "Drew's terrible baking streak continues."

Kyle looked around the kitchen and at him and Allie for a good, long minute.

"Certainly looks like it. You better be looking for a new liberal arts elective for next semester, because there is no way Mrs. Richards is passing you if you are this much of a disaster." Kyle walked up the stairs, gym bag in tow and the moment was gone.

March 3, 2012

Allie never did mention his sloppy attempt to kiss her that day. Drew had always been grateful for that. He started walking back to the designated room when he stepped on a shoelace. He bent over to fix the lace and the small piece of paper he had tucked into his suit jacket for safe keeping fell on the floor in front of him. Once again, he couldn't seem to help himself. While Drew knew it was a terrible idea, he still reached forward to grab the paper. He opened it and read it right there on bended knee.

Allie,

Sweet Allie. Today as you become my wife, I have to tell you all the reasons why I love you. I love you because you care more about magnolias than getting dirt on your clothes. I love you because you can make anything look good, including having flour all over your hair. I love you because you make me better. And with you the world and everything in it just feels a little bit brighter. So, I vow to you today that I will help you remember how much I love you each and every day of my life.

And for a moment after he was finished rereading the short declaration, Drew could not move. He felt paralyzed. He had heard of people getting cold feet before a wedding, but he had never heard of anyone being petrified. Too bad he did not have any mandrake root. That would have been a sure way to snap him out of this feeling. But, being a muggle, he did not have access to such things. So, he merely decided to pace around the space to calm his nerves. He quickly tucked the paper back into his inside suit pocket. Drew took deep breaths in and out and closed his eyes. He needed another swig of whiskey. But now, he did not want to go back to that room.

I love her.

He just needed to keep repeating that like a mantra. Drew knew that today that was all that mattered. That he could cling onto that one simple truth and allow it to tamp down all the other emotions he was feeling. He took one last deep breath and turned to walk back to the room. Suddenly, the rest of the groom's party walked into the kitchen.

"Alright gentlemen. Time to take our places," Fred called out.

* * *

Allie daintily brushed her fingers down the pearl colored taffeta fabric of her princess cut gown. She tentatively grabbed the crook of her father's left elbow. Her head moved like a beach telescope scanning the yard. The whole place was transformed into a beautiful venue for her perfect wedding. Allie wasn't the type of little girl who over fantasized about her wedding day. At seven, she had been far more interested in helping Donkey Kong save his country. At ten she had been absorbed in reading about the wizarding world of Harry Potter. Then, at thirteen she had been hit by cupid, bitten by the love bug, or whatever you call it.

Allie looked up and her eyes fell on Drew. She smiled as she thought back to that summer a decade ago. She remembered how furious she was with him for breaking the branches of the magnolia bush. The beautiful spring flowers were still her favorite part about the home where she spent her teenage years. Allie remembered how quickly her fury had died down when she saw Drew sporting a Hogwarts baseball cap the next day. They had become fast friends and he was her first love. Allie felt a little tickle from the giggle that caught in her throat as she thought about the love note she wrote when she was a teen.

Drew,

I was so worried when my parents moved our family to Ohio. I left behind a lot of good friends. Now, I think it's the best thing that ever happened. This move led me to meeting you. You make me care less about saving Princess Peach and care more about making myself look like a princess. I am so excited that you're a Potterhead like me. We have already managed a lot of mischief together. I just want you to know that I am falling for you. I hope you feel the same way too.

Allie

She smiled thinking about how fortunate she was that the first boy she had fallen in love with was the same man who was her best friend.

The sound of the violinist playing The Wedding March brought Allie back to the moment. She moved slowly next to her father, taking the time to absorb everything and everyone. Everyone was standing and looking back at her. Their hair and clothing were blowing along with the slight breeze in the air. The feeling was magical, like she was floating on a cloud. Then she looked back to the altar, locking her gaze on the groom. The broad grin on his face caused hot tears to sting her eyes. Allie held her composure until she reached the end of the aisle and she saw tears on her father's face. A few tears slipped as she hugged him before he gave her hand to her future husband.

* * *

The next thing Drew knew, everyone was lined up and everyone was just waiting for Allie to walk down the aisle. His heartbeat was echoing in his eardrums. He could feel his legs wobbling and was trying to remember the pastor's brief rundown on not locking his knees during the ceremony. Then he spotted Allie, and all other thoughts were eclipsed by just one.

She looks beautiful.

Drew focused in on her face and that gorgeous, genuine smile of hers. It was a good reminder to himself that he needed to smile too. It also reminded him of all the many doodles of that very face that ended up on the side of his architecture plans in college. So, he thought of all those silly doodles from a few years ago, tried to smile, and willed his legs not to collapse out from underneath him. The ceremony began and he could not pay attention to a single word. Until he heard the pastor say, "It is time for the lovely couple to exchange their vows."

As if he were a puppet on strings, Drew reached into his suit pocket, pulled out the small piece of paper from earlier, handed it to his brother Kyle and then stepped back into his place in line up as best man.

"Allie. Sweet Allie..."

Listening to his brother recite the words, words that could have just have easily come directly from his lips, was one of the most painful things he had ever done in his life. But, he would do anything for Allie. Anything, including letting her marry the man she loved. Even if that man was his brother.

Once in a Blue Moon

A Kip and the Peggies Adventure

By Charlee Kressbach

Kip was still digging into his breakfast of pecan pancakes flooded with maple syrup and melted butter, when Chaud, his godfather, heaved a sigh, patted his plaid shirted belly and pushed away from the table. "Thanks for the breakfast, May, I can't eat another bite." He approached his wife, wrapping her in a hug and giving her a quick sticky peck on the cheek. May giggled and fruitlessly tried to wipe the gooey kiss from her face.

Kip, whose cheeks were stuffed with the buttery goodness, nodded his compliments to the chef.

May spoke up. "According to the paper, there's a blue moon tonight. I thought you'd like to know."

Chaud slowly tipped his hat back. "Blue moon, huh? " He grunted, rubbing his neck as if shaking off an imaginary chill.

Kip swallowed and looked at May. "What's so special about a blue moon?"

"According to the article, blue moons are technically the second full moon occurring in any given month. Some folk believe they evoke special powers. But that seems to be myth and legend," May explained, fluffing her apron as if to dispel any crazy thoughts.

Kip helped clear the table. He took the stairs to his bedroom two at a time. Scanning his library, he pulled out one reference book on astronomy and a star atlas that his Uncle Ralph gave him years ago.

"Blue moon," he muttered to himself as he riffled through the pages. The entry confirmed May's abridged explanation. "According to the ancient beliefs, the blue moon was a time for mythical creatures to celebrate. Many people claim to have seen fairies and other supernatural beings during the light of the blue moon."

He leaned out his bedroom window to confirm the fact that Larkspur and Pansy, the winged horses' fairy caretakers, had already taken the peggies to the field for their daily exercise. Grabbing his notebook and colored pencils, Kip bolted down the stairs, stopped in the kitchen for a snack and ran to the field. It was a clear, almost cloudless day with bright sunshine. He saw the peggies silhouetted against the deep blue sky cavorting with each other. Pansy and Larkspur's son, Thyme, was playing tag with the winged horses. Thyme was often tagged 'it' because the horses were much faster and adept at the game.

Kip flopped down in his usual spot underneath the trees next to the field where Larkspur and Pansy had already set up camp. He quickly sketched Pansy, who was busy at work with her lap full of meadow flowers: daisies, feverfew, sweet pea, and yarrow. She deftly braided the flower stems into circlets with bright ribbons attached. Pansy flapped her wings and flew over to her daughter, Lily. The flowery crown was dangling from her hand.

Kip was distracted by the arrival of one of his favorite winged horses. Dew was the first baby winged horse born to his herd and held a special place in his heart. Kip patted the mare's aqua coat and scratched her yellow mane. Mist, Dew's mother, spotted him right away and approached, her dark blue mane and tail streaming behind her. She was keeping up with the stallion, Mistral's, muscular tan and yellow flanks. Mist zoomed in to perch on Kip's shoulder. She pawed his shirt material and nibbled lightly on his ear.

"Here you go, you little beggars," said Kip in a kindly way, handing them each a piece of apple peel.

He only had a few moments before the rest of the herd deluged him for treats. He watched as Stratus, the pinto mare, approached with her brown wings flashing in the sunlight. Sirocco, the stallion, was winning the race to Kip, the peggie's red wings slicing through the air. Kip looked for Nimbus, the green mare and Zephyr, the black stallion. They were gliding with Cirrus, whose white wings were almost hidden in the clouds.

"Larkspur, what do you know about the blue moon?" asked Kip.

"There's one tonight. Our preparations are almost complete!" Larkspur had a big goofy grin on his face.

"Preparations?" Kip asked, looking still at Larkspur for answers. Out of the corner of his eye he watched Pansy and Lily. Lily was shaking her head as Pansy tried to give her the flowery tiara.

"Blue moons are special for us," confirmed Larkspur. "It's like a Valentine's Day. Fairy couples who have fallen in love during the year get engaged in a special ceremony. We were hoping you'd let us take the peggies with us to the celebration tonight in your Uncle Elias's garden."

Kip couldn't think of a good reason why not, so he nodded his approval. Soon the conversation was cut short by the rest of the demanding herd of miniature winged horses, all of whom were extremely fond of apple peelings.

Pansy rejoined them, continuing to braid the pink, yellow and white flower stems with the ribbons. "Is anyone from your family getting engaged?" asked Kip, still curious about the event.

"No, not really," answered Larkspur, blushing. He reached out for Pansy's hand. "Pansy and I are going to renew our vows." Pansy leaned over, kissing her husband affectionately on the cheek. Mistral, the stallion, quickly thrust his muzzle between the two fairies, cutting the romantic kiss short. Pansy pushed the troublemaker away, giggling.

Kip noticed Lily, Larkspur and Pansy's daughter, still sitting by herself looking sullen. "Where's Val?" Kip asked. Val and Lily were inseparable friends. Pansy and Larkspur looked a bit uncomfortable.

"Lily's upset because Val has found herself a young man. They are going to get engaged tonight during the ceremony.

"Kip heard a song buzzing around in his head, something about love.

Pansy finished the circlet she was working on, jumped up and flew to her daughter. She gathered Lily in her arms. "When I was young, I had a really good friend. Her name was Posey. No matter what hare-brained scheme I thought up, she was my partner in crime. We had some crazy adventures. There were also times when we were both grounded for crossing the line. When Posey found the love of her life, I was devastated. They were betrothed at the blue moon festival and married a short time later. Posey moved with her husband to a fairy colony west of the woods, leaving Elias's garden for good. I never saw her again, even though we promised to write and keep in touch." Pansy had tears in her eyes.

"What happened to you?" Lily asked.

Pansy sighed. "I was so depressed I spent a lot of time by myself, until this fairy kept getting in my way." She pointed with her thumb, giving Larkspur a friendly glare. "Every time I turned around he was there! It was infuriating. He kept pestering me until I finally said yes. We were betrothed the next blue moon." She looked lovingly over to Larkspur, who wore a wide grin full of memories of their courtship.

Kip cleared his throat. This definitely felt like way too much information. He rose. "Best be going. Maybe I'll see you later." He left the remaining pile of apple peels on Larkspur's lap.

"Kip, why don't you join us at moonrise? Elias is usually there on the back porch enjoying the festivities," Larkspur offered.

"Okay!" Kip left with a smile and a wave.

On the way back home, he stopped at Chaud's workshop. "Chaud? What do you know about blue moons?" Chaud looked a bit uncomfortable, turning his back and rubbing the nape of his neck, trying to distract Kip by pretending he was too busy to talk. Kip persevered, making eye contact and standing with his hands on his hips.

"Well, I don't know much, but I have seen strange things happen on the night of the blue moon." Chaud scratched his bristly chin. "Do you remember when your Uncle Wellington and his family came to stay? I invited your cousins to go fishing." Kip nodded. He remembered going fishing with them that time. "I went out to dig night crawlers in the kitchen garden. There was a blue moon that night. The worms like to surface during a full moon, especially if the dew is heavy. That night they were so plentiful, I didn't have to dig them. I just picked those nice, big, fat worms up off the grass. That wasn't the strangest thing, though. The worms, instead of being brown with lighter, tan underbellies, glowed in all the colors of the rainbow. I thought my eyes were playing tricks on me."

Chaud pushed back his hat and rubbed his forehead with the back of his hand. "I put them in a bait can with a bit of moss and wondered how I would explain brightly colored worms to you and the boys. The next morning when I retrieved the bait, bamboo rods, and fishing creel from the shed, the worms were their normal brown color. I couldn't explain it. Maybe it was a dream." Chaud shrugged. "Strange things happen when there's a blue moon," he muttered, turning away.

After dinner Kip went to his room. He opened his bedroom window and stared at the empty stable. Larkspur's family had already taken the horses to Elias's garden. Kip knew he wouldn't completely relax until his winged horses returned to their stables. He looked toward the east, where the moon was just beginning to rise.

Kip grabbed his camera and sketch book. He loped through the twilight to his Uncle Elias' Victorian mansion, skirting the main house and entering the summer kitchen through the doorway. Elias was already there tapping his foot to the fairy music.

"Hallo, KC," Elias greeted his nephew with a smile. "Join me."

Kip sat down and placed his camera on the flat porch rail. He noticed a smoldering pot of herbs on the rail in front of his uncle.

"What's that?" Kip wondered.

"It's a smudge pot. This time of night there are biting insects. When my father was alive, he would sit out here smoking a big stinky cigar to keep the mosquitoes away. Since I don't smoke, the fairies provide me with this smudge pot with green herbs. The insects don't like the smoke from the burning vegetation." Elias reached over and waved his hand, dispersing the tendrils of smoke.

As usual, the fairies took their celebrations seriously. The orchard was decorated with tiny lantern lights. The large fairy orchestra did not need speakers; the tunes could be heard throughout the garden. The gazebo was beautifully festooned in fresh flowers. It was here that Tulip and Twig, the matriarch and patriarch of the fairies, held court.

Kip grabbed his sketch book and quickly drew the orchard. His attention was drawn to the activity by the gazebo. He watched as a young boy and girl fairy approached Tulip and Twig. Kip could not hear what was said, but could hear the applause and congratulations from the crowd as Tulip placed the flowered wreath on the head of the girl fairy and Twig a similar wreath on the boy's head. The newly blessed couple flew off holding hands for their first dance as the other fairies threw apple blossom petals over them.

Kip was fascinated. He grabbed his camera and tried to take pictures of the event, but he knew that due to the low light and elusive nature of the fairies, the pictures probably would not turn out.

He noticed that Lily approached the porch carrying a fresh sprig of sage. She placed it on the smudge pot, backed up to the fire and waggled her wings, causing the smoke to curl into the orchard. "Thanks, Lily," Kip said. "Are you having fun?"

Lily shrugged but then turned away as she heard her name called. Kip heard a boy fairy ask her to dance. Lily smiled as she flew off.

Kip looked up when he heard cheering. He recognized the silhouettes of Pansy and Larkspur approaching the gazebo. Tulip greeted her granddaughter with smiles and hugs. Twig shook Larkspur's hand. As the ceremony continued, Kip could see Pansy's smile. Larkspur's smile matched hers. They sealed their renewal of vows with a kiss and lowered their heads so they could receive the flowered crowns from the officiants. They were engulfed in apple blossom petals as they whisked off to dance

Now the celebration began in earnest. Food magically appeared on the tables, the music became peppier and the orchard was soon filled with dancing fairies.

The orchestra was playing a version of the song, Blue Moon. Once in a while a fairy would look up and point at the moon. When Kip looked up he noticed bats winging above the orchard, eating their fill of insects. His precious peggies were busy giving the fairy children rides. Thyme, the gatekeeper for the rides, had a line of fairy children behind him patiently waiting their turn. The peggies would return to Thyme every time he raised his arm.

Kip's Uncle Elias rose from his chair. "Excuse me, Kip, it's time for me to turn in. These celebrations usually last to the wee hours."

"I was thinking about going, too. Thanks for letting me watch with you." Kip gave his uncle a sideways hug, then left the porch for home. Retracing his steps through the woodland, he jumped when an owl hooted loudly and flew over the path.

He could still hear the fairies celebrating. An orchestra was playing and the notes drifted up as if riding the moonbeams. The whole yard and garden were bright as daylight. The kitchen garden was well established with pristine rows of wax beans, cucumbers and hills of squash. With Chaud in charge of the garden, the weeds did not stand a chance. Kip looked more closely at the tended rows. Something was not right.

Taking up his camera, he moved closer to the eerie looking garden. The composting smell of horse manure sparred with the sweet smell of the honeysuckle. The soil was glowing in unnatural colors of pink, blue, orange, green and purple. It seemed to pulse with life. The earthworms were on the surface, just like Chaud remembered.

Kip snapped multiple photos of the garden.

"Kip!" a fairy voice shouted.

Kip looked up and saw the peggies and their fairy caretakers returning home. "What are you doing?"

"Do you see them?" asked Kip, pointing at the glowing worms.

Pansy giggled, "Oh Kip, haven't you seen this before? When we muck out the stables, we pile the manure and straw along the paths of the garden as fertilizer. Peggie poop glows under the blue moon's rays."

"I wonder if it will show up on film," Kip remarked. He was glad it was dark enough to hide his blush.

Good Vibrations

By David McFarland

"You're in room two," said Nurse Vickerson. Her white Keds sneakers squeaked as she took slow steps down the Apex Care Clinic.

"Thank you. Do you know if Doctor Peterson is here?" replied Olivia. She pressed down on her maternity top that she'd purchased at Mommy and Me!, a strip mall shop designed to appeal to the mature, pregnant mother.

"He got a call from the hospital and it could be quite a wait," stated Nurse Vickerson. She sniffed the air and could still smell the hidden diaper in room three that had been pitched by a mother of two children under five or ten minutes ago.

"Oh, okay, well, thanks," said Olivia. With her left hand, she twisted her wedding ring back and forth.

"Stop. That's Room Three. You're in the next one, Room Two," barked the nurse. She tapped her white Keds as Olivia slowly turned around.

"Sorry, I guess we are just a little nervous today," said Keith, Olivia's husband. He opened the door to Room Two and waited as Olivia waddled in.

"If that's the case then why didn't you reschedule like the office asked you to?" said the nurse. She watched as Keith helped Olivia sit on the examination table.

"No, it's me. I just wanted to hear something," Olivia said. She lifted her face and let her eyes rest on the nurse as if she had all the answers.

"When was your last prenatal visit?" questioned Nurse Vickerson. She snatched Olivia's chart out of the rack and slapped it on the counter of the examination room.

"I know you're right. We should have waited. It's just that I didn't feel her moving around and being seven months pregnant and all..."

"Excuse me? There it is," said Nurse Vickerson. She blew a fallen curl out of her face that had dropped when she bent down to look at the chart. "Your last prenatal visit was only two weeks ago."

"There just wasn't anything tonight. Not even a vibration," Olivia whispered. Tiny tears formed in her left eye and trickled onto her eyelashes.

"You should have been feeling a lot more by now. Just have a seat and someone will be with you shortly," said Nurse Vickerson. She picked up the chart, shuffled the papers and placed it back in the rack.

"Keith, can you explain it better? I just don't seem to have the right words," Olivia said. In her throat, a lump formed that made it difficult for her to speak about this topic.

"Every night, after supper, around seven, Olivia gets a...oh, I don't know what you'd call it. Maybe just a slight nudge, or like she said, a vibration."

"Are you charting this?"

Olivia interrupted and said, "No, it was just a pattern. We called it our baby time, when Keith would know he could feel Kylie."

"Megan," said Keith. "Her name is Megan"

"You need to be charting out patterns like this, especially at your age. I would think you would know."

"Know what?" said Olivia. The slump in her back suddenly disappeared and she sat up straight. With her right hand, she wiped her eyes.

"Why don't you just lie down here and the doctor will be with you shortly," said Nurse Vickerson as she shut the door behind her.

"Keith, what did she mean by that?"

"Olivia, stop. Don't let her get to you. She's just upset that we got in for an appointment," said Keith. He rubbed his hands together and they made a scraping sound.

"She means because I am thirty-five doesn't she?"

"No, it doesn't mean that at all. She's just having a bad day. It has nothing to do with you or baby Megan."

"Let's go. I don't want to be here if they don't want me to be here," said Olivia. She swung her legs off the examination table and groaned when a sudden sharp pain shot up her back.

"Where would we go? Back home?" said Keith. He rushed over and held out his hand to steady her.

"Let's go to the emergency room."

"Olivia, we can't. The first question they are going to ask us is who is our obstetrician."

"So, we tell them, they'll understand."

"No, they'll keep us there until the next morning when Dr. Peterson does his morning rounds."

"Maybe that'd be better," said Olivia. She took a small step toward the door.

"We have a deductible of $5,000. We would end up paying the whole thing when they shove you into a hospital bed just to get the same appointment with Dr. Peterson we are getting now," said Keith. He glanced up from his chair to the buzzing fluorescent lights as if they had the answer.

"Is it all about money?"

"No, fine. Let's go," said Keith. He walked ahead of Olivia and opened the door.

"No, we'll wait. It's probably just me being weird anyway," said Olivia. She turned around and headed back to the table

"No, it's like we talked about. Megan is just being stubborn. It runs in your family."

Olivia smiled, looked at the floor and avoided Keith's eyes when she said, "I shouldn't have painted the nursery. I just couldn't stand the trim."

"I would have been home shortly and I could have done it," Keith said and put his hand out to help her get on the table.

Olivia pushed his hand away. "Really? Is that why the refrigerator shelf for the breast milk hasn't been replaced yet?"

"I'll get to it."

"Peach and apples. Whoever heard of fruits for a nursery border," said Olivia. She used both hands on the edge of the table to hoist herself up.

"I could have painted over the border."

"That's the lazy way. I want everything in that nursery to be perfect."

"It will be," said Keith. The examination room door swung open and Dr. Peterson strolled in.

"Hi, folks. How ya doing today?"

"Good, I just wanted to come a week early because I haven't felt anything since yesterday at noon and…" Olivia said and stopped. Dr. Peterson had moved toward Keith and had avoided her eyes.

"And how's dad doing? Learning how to put together baby cribs?"

"It's a challenge. But it's like my wife was saying, we are concerned about the lack of activity."

"Oh, now folks. Stop. Babies do their own thing. You better get used to your daughter having a mind of her own."

Olivia spoke up and said, "I think it's more than that. I read on the internet that the umbilical cord can get wrapped around a baby's neck at seven months."

Doctor Peterson buried his hands in the pockets of his immaculate white coat. He scolded mostly Olivia and said, "Now, there are a lot of things that can happen. But you know what? They don't. Most babies in most situations come out just fine no matter how much Mom and Dad worry."

"Okay," said Olivia in a small and shallow voice.

"So. Why don't we just see how things are and we will see you at your next biweekly prenatal appointment."

Olivia turned her head toward her husband. "Keith," she said in a low and firm tone.

"We want another ultrasound," said Keith. He straightened his back so he stood at his full six foot height.

"You will, next week when we run the entire works. It's just that today we are a little more behind than normal. Chart what you notice and we'll have more to discuss at the next appointment."

"Keith," Olivia said and bit her bottom lip.

"We want one. Today. Before we leave. Or..." Keith swallowed and said, "We will go to the emergency room and find a physician who will do it."

"Keith, no, we won't do that. Dr. Peterson is almost part of our family." Olivia cooed in a higher pitched voice.

"That's true. I delivered your sister's baby. Lucy um...um..."

"Appleton."

"That's right Appleton."

"And that's why we're here. My sister put posts on Facebook so all our friends and relatives could see what amazing care she received."

"Well, thank you."

"And we just want some of that extra care that you give. That's what brought us here in the first place."

"I'll have Nurse Vickerson come in here and run the ultrasound," Dr. Peterson quickly said.

"Thank you," Olivia chirped as the door shut.

Keith focused his gaze on her and glared. He said, "Why would you say that to him?"

"We're getting the ultrasound."

"You didn't have to suck up to him like that."

"You're right. You should've said something."

"Do you know what I wanted to say? Fine, screw us over. We don't have money so we can wait. I guess we can just go to the parking lot and I'll shine the car headlights on you and see what I can figure out."

Olivia patted down her ill-fitting maternity top. She quietly said, "I don't want a scene."

"I don't either. I just want some answers."

"Keith. Stop. This is the man whose hands are going to be in my body multiple times."

Keith snorted and stared at the poster of a happy drooling baby across from him.

Olivia started to ease herself into a lying position. She said, "Seriously, unless you're volunteering to have a little extra encounter with Dr. Peterson's latex gloves, bring it down."

"Right, okay," said Keith and folded his arms.

"Hold my hand," said Olivia. She held out her hand and dangled her fingers in Keith's direction.

Keith slid the battered orange plastic chair next to her and let his fingers be intertwined with hers. "When we get home, I'll get that border down," he whispered.

"With a ladder, not the kitchen chair. I don't need to worry about you, too."

This quiet moment ended with the door being flung open. Nurse Vickerson shoved an unwieldy ultrasound machine into the tiny room. After it careened to a stop, she set up her supplies and smeared cool gel on Olivia's stomach. Olivia winced as the ball of the ultrasound, which looked like an old fashioned deodorant roll on, rode across the oversized bump in her belly.

"Hmm."

"What's wrong?" asked Olivia. She squeezed the sides of the table.

"I didn't say anything is wrong. Sometimes we play *hide and go seek* when we use this ultrasound."

"Can you explain what we're seeing?" Keith asked. His voice raised an entire octave.

"It's not so much what we are seeing, it's what we're not," said Nurse Vickerson as she peered at the screen.

"What can't you see?" said Olivia inaudibly. It took every ounce of her self-discipline not to move.

"I'll have the doctor come back in and explain it to you," said the nurse in a subdued voice. She pushed the machine out and slowly pulled the door closed.

Once she left, Olivia said, "It's like I told you. I didn't feel anything all throughout the day."

"It's going to be okay."

"But that's what I told myself. It's okay. When Keith gets home, we'll have our family time. Everything will be fine. But it's not."

"A broken machine doesn't mean anything. For all we know--"

Doctor Peterson pushed the door open. "Folks, sorry to say this..." he said in a deep and low utterance.

"Oh my God," Olivia tearfully gasped.

"Well now, it may not be anything to be concerned about but we want to make sure..."

"Make sure of what?" Keith demanded. He repositioned his chair to face the doctor.

"We can't find the heartbeat."

"Oh my God," Olivia sobbed into her hands.

"It doesn't mean you have to be concerned. We're going to send it to California to be reviewed."

"We have to come back next week?" Keith asked with hope.

"No, nothing like that. They'll review and we'll know tonight if something on our end is acting up or if it's more than that."

"Wait, let me understand what you're saying..." said Keith. He stood up as if direct confrontation could solve this problem.

"All I am saying is, let's wait. We need to know more before we decide anything," said Doctor Peterson before he left the room.

"Decide about what?" Keith shouted at the closed door.

"Keith, it's just like my Aunt Vera."

"No, it's not. She was in her forties; you're only 35 years old."

"My mother was with her when she found out."

"I'm with you now and it's all going to be alright," said Keith. He laid his hand on top of her open hand and felt her sweat on it.

"They forced her to deliver the dead baby."

"I'm sure they didn't do that. There must've been a better way."

"No. Back then they told her that way was the best way for her body." Olivia stopped and then when she started again her voice became mechanical. She said, "She had to go through five hours of labor to deliver the baby."

"We have a better doctor. That couldn't happen to us," said Keith. He picked up her hand with his and kissed it.

"Her doctor was an Ivy League doctor and it still happened to her"

"That's not gonna happen to us," Keith said. He rubbed her hand against the red hot fire in his cheeks.

"You don't know."

"Why don't you practice your Lamaze breathing exercises to calm yourself?" he said and lowered her hand.

"Why don't you stop trying to control what I feel."

"I'm not. I just don't want to see you get worked up over nothing."

"Nothing?" Olivia said. The rawness of her throat from the fear she swallowed that night ached. She slowly said, "Her little baby Glen was buried in a coffin."

"For a seven month old baby?"

"You wouldn't do that?"

"I'm not gonna have to. Everything is going to be fine. Just breathe," said Keith. He sat up straight again and looked her in the eye.

Olivia returned his attention. "I wanted to give you a baby boy," she whispered.

"You know that doesn't matter to me."

"She knew. My baby girl knew that I wanted a boy."

"No, that's not true. She knows how much we love her. Think how much we talk and sing to her. She has to know."

"My body betrayed me because it knew. It knew I wanted a boy," Olivia said. Her entire body trembled after this sentence.

Keith moved closer to her. He wrapped his arms around Olivia. She let his body gently sway her back-and-forth.

Olivia said so only Keith could hear her, "If everything turns out okay, I swear to God I'm going to be the best mother ever."

"You already are," said Keith. He held her close as she closed her eyes

"Why is it taking so long?" said Olivia and opened her eyes. She listened to the buzz of the fluorescent lights

"We want it to take a long time. We want them to be as thorough as possible."

"Keith, what time is it?"

"4:30."

"We've been here eight hours?"

"Do you know what this reminds me of?" said Keith. He nuzzled his chin closer to her.

"What?"

"That Beach Boys song."

"No, not the Beach Boys. Nothing you can say about the Beach Boys can have anything remotely to do with my--our--pregnancy."

"No, wait. It's that song, 'Good Vibrations'," said Keith. He started to untangle himself from Oliva.

"What?"

"You need them. WE need them."

"Okay, and.." Olivia said distracted.

"And I studied this in music appreciation class in college. There is a break in the song where everyone thinks it's Brian Wilson but it's really Carl Wilson, because he has a voice that, well, as it was explained to me, reaches angelic heights."

"Okay, fine."

"Or, maybe that's 'God Only Knows' where Carl Wilson sings."

"Maybe you should just sing it for me so I know what this conversation is about."

"No, I can't."

"I'm doing my part laying here, you need to do your part. Bring it on, music man."

Keith stood up, moved in front of her and blinked twice. In a high pitched falsetto, he sang the wrong words: "I want them, I need them, good vibrations."

"Oh, you're right. You can't sing it. It's more like this." Then, Olivia sat up and hesitated, wavered as if unsure she should sing or not, before she sang in a voice a full pitch higher, "I want them, I need them, good vibrations."

A toothy grin spread across Keith's face as he, in as low a baritone as he could manage, harmonized, "I want them, I need them, good vibrations."

The door room sprung open and banged against the wall.

Nurse Vickerson tiredly said, "The two of you can go home. Your baby is alive. The specialist in California said our machine is acting up."

"Good, good, good, good vibrations!" Keith shouted loud enough that if there was anyone in the next three rooms over they could hear. He left Olivia, stomped his feet toward Nurse Vickerson, grabbed her hands and spun her around three times. He looked like a happy Labrador puppy throwing around his white toy Bunny.

Olivia smiled and whispered to her stomach, "She's giving me expectations."

After Keith let her go, Nurse Vickerson steadied herself, laughed and asked, "What's your daughter's name?"

Keith beamed. He joyfully proclaimed, "Megan. It's Megan and it's because of that baby I've got good vibrations."

"Kylie," Olivia firmly said.

"Whose Kylie?" asked Nurse Vickerson in confusion.

"Our baby."

"Megan," Keith goofily asserted.

"Okay. The two of you need to just go home and get some sleep," said Nurse Vickerson. As she did so, she realized that there was still a tangy nastiness coming from a diaper in Room Three.

Keith went to his orange battered chair, sat down and sighed. He looked and Olivia, placed his hand on her stomach and said, "I've got my good vibrations back."

Olivia smiled and thought, *baby time is back.*

Blind Love

By Katey Morgan

I spend every weekend with a girlfriend I'm trying to break up with.

Seven months ago, I moved over an hour away to drop a hint she never chose to pick up. It was Saturday morning and we were eating breakfast quietly in my kitchen.

"Don't you think it's time I just move in?" Rae bluntly asked.

Here we go.

I quickly cleared my throat and placed my elbows on the table to move my unfinished plate out of the way. I sheepishly met her gaze. Her face immediately shifted to concern and a defensive tone awoke in her words.

"Why can't we ever talk about this, Leo?" She began to speak again when my cellphone's text alert went off. "Perfect timing. Now you have an excuse to walk away." Her dark brown eyes narrowed as she awaited my move.

Annoyed, I scooted the chair back loudly against my kitchen tile floor and stood. Avoiding eye contact with her, I turned to leave the kitchen toward the hallway and attempted to stomp my bare feet on the cold tile floor as I left.

Perfect timing no doubt.

Being a broadband technician sometimes meant weekend emergencies that would require me to pull out the work laptop and do a few things for a couple hours. This was pretty sporadic, but often enough where Rae became use to it. Only this time, the text message wasn't from my boss; it was from Mary.

Mary and I worked together four years ago and almost dated before I met Rae. We always kept in contact, Rae just never knew it. I didn't have social media so that helped eliminate the need for me to explain any of my female contacts. Not that I was a bad guy to Rae. I never touched anyone else after I met her. It's just Mary was my best friend. I could talk to her about anything. She even knew my complicated feelings towards Rae and was trying to help me figure out how to handle them.

I quickly responded back and then set Mary's message thread to hidden notifications. I could hear Rae's footsteps coming down the hardwood floor towards the bedroom where I stood. I set my phone down on my night stand as she entered the room, her eyes red as if she was on the brink of crying at any moment. Her long, black hair matched her jet-black eyeliner and lipstick.

"Rae..." I lingered and pulled her close to my chest to hold her. "I love spending time with you," I lied. "You know I'm just trying to get settled financially before we make that step."

I had to lie to her. The truth would crush her completely and I was way too scared to do that right now. I had never initiated a break-up before in my life and I had no idea how to do it nicely. No one had ever done it nicely to me. I began slowly caressing her smooth, straight hair. I could smell her lavender and lemon body oil. The same scent when I first met her at a Spiritual and Holistic store downtown. I was there to set up their new internet and she was there giving tarot card readings.

She looked up at me, sighed and began kissing me.

* * *

"So, I told her to forget it. I'm not going to paint on a canvas that small. It's not worth the stress or the money she was going to pay me. I'm so glad I did it. Now I need a good selenite bath to get rid of this energy." Rae was smiling at me through her phone during our normal Wednesday night Skype video call.

"Yeah," I said, not fully listening.

"Leo, what's on your mind? It's really distracting me from enjoying our conversation." Rae's annoyance was displayed by the raising of her right eyebrow and resting of her head in her left hand as she continued to keep her gaze at me on her phone.

I leaned my head back on my pillow and glanced up at the ceiling for a moment.

"Leo?" Rae's tone changed from annoyance to concern.

Returning my gaze back to the phone I said quickly, "I'm on my way to see you."

"What?! It's an hour drive and it's almost 11 o'clock." Rae's rebuttal caught me off guard. I didn't really expect her to deter me from coming over.

Regardless of her reaction, I couldn't break up with her over Skype. It was just too wrong. Getting up from my bed, still holding the phone in front of my face I explained, "I have something really important we need to discuss. I want to do it in person. I'm on my way."

Rae's eyes lit up and I knew what she was thinking. "Oh! Um, well, I will be here ready for you!" Her smile made me queasy. I hung up before she or I could say anything else.

*　*　*

My black Chevy Tahoe slowly pulled into Rae's apartment building parking lot. It had new landscaping and the children's park equipment had been refurbished. I hadn't been here once since I had moved. I not only moved an hour away from her but also made her come to me every weekend.

God, I'm a prick.

My nerves were beginning to get the best of me. Frantically, I turned off the car's ignition and allowed the darkness of the midnight hour to consume the inside of my car. I sat in the darkness for a few moments debating how I wanted to initiate the conversation. I'd driven all this way, I couldn't just fold and let her think this conversation was about her moving in with me. I took a deep breath and prepared myself. Nodding slowly, I heard myself sort it all out in my head.

She's going to be happy when she first sees you. Stay cold. Don't kiss her or make eye contact. Stay standing and leave your shoes on, but ask her to sit. Get straight to the point. Say you don't have feelings anymore and have come to tell her it's over. She'll cry. A lot. Let her cry, just don't comfort her. Say you're sorry and that you hope you can remain friends. She may get pissed about that but let that be your parting words as you walk out of her apartment. Then haul your ass home.

I took another deep inhale and exhale and then exited the car. I cautiously walked up to her apartment floor and stood in front of door 4C. As I lifted my fist to knock, the door abruptly opened. Rae stood before me in black lingerie. Her hair was down with make-up freshly painted on her face. Her eyes were seductive and her smile was choking me. I heard our song playing on her iPod in her bedroom.

"Hey baby..." she purred and stepped aside to let me in. She began to touch my back with her long nails, lightly scratching me. I felt my body freeze and become rigid. Lavender and lemon suddenly was the most repulsive scent I'd ever inhaled.

"Rae, go sit down on the couch. I need to tell you something."

"Oh, I know what you're going to tell me and I can't wait to celebrate it." She walked seductively around my body to face me. "Tell me—"

I grabbed her shoulders and stared sternly into her eyes. Interrupting her I said, "Rae, I said SIT DOWN!" My voice was raised and sharp and I felt my heart race. At this point I was just getting pissed off. She always thought she could read my mind and was ten steps ahead of me because of her "intuitive abilities."

She jerked her head back as her eyes widened in surprise. "Okay," she whispered. She awkwardly walked to her couch and sat down with her hands rested on her lap. The smell of lavender and lemon left with her.

"I came here to tell you in person that I no longer have feelings for you," I said robotically, just as I had rehearsed in my head a moment earlier. "It's over between us."

My words filled the room and hung in the air like smoke from a cigar. Rae's eyes started to tear and her chest began to rise and fall rapidly. She lowered her head for a moment, closing her eyes and letting a few tear drops fall into her hands on her lap. She then returned her gaze back to me and stood up. Her stare was stabbing my face and if there ever was a competition for evil, dirty looks, she would've won the crown. She quickly walked towards me and I instinctively took a few steps back.

She grabbed my face between her hands and glared deeply into my blue eyes. Her eyes narrowed and she said softly, "You will regret this." She let go and opened the door for me to leave.

I stood there awkwardly for a moment and then regained my composure. "I—I hope we can still be friends," I mumbled as I hurried out the door.

Her apartment door slammed behind me as I continued quickly down the staircase and out of the apartment building. My hands shook violently as I tried to unlock my car and put the keys into the ignition.

Once I started the vehicle, I took a few deep breaths and began to laugh. "Holy shit, that was so horrible!" I continued to laugh, now throwing my head back. "I thought she was going to *kill* me!"

That's when I noticed a full moon in the night sky. "Huh," I said, "Well, full moons and new beginnings, I guess." I laughed and sang along to an old eighties rock station the entire drive home.

* * *

"Wait, wait," Mary giggled as she took another sip of her cranberry and vodka cocktail. "You drove a whole hour in the middle of the night just to break up with her?!" Her laughter grew as she closed her eyes. Her short, red curls bounced as she slowly shook her head in disbelief.

"I had to get it over with," I laughed. "It was such a weight on my shoulders and I told you I had never broken up with someone before. I was always the one getting dumped!" I took a gulp of my beer and smiled while I watched Mary's lips part to put a long, thin cigarette in her mouth.

"That had to have been so awkward, wow! I give you props, though. Most men would've just sent a text and moved on." She rolled her eyes and rummaged through her purse for a lighter.

"I'm really glad we could meet for dinner. It's been way too long," I said taking the lighter out of my jeans pocket. She leaned towards me with the cigarette in her mouth, gently placing her left hand on my thigh and momentarily meeting my eyes. She let the flame engulf the cigarette for a few seconds then drew back.

"I know, I've missed you," she winked.

Was that an attempt to flirt?

We continued the rest of the evening laughing and chatting over dinner. She had taken a job about fifteen minutes away from my new place and was looking for a condo. I offered to let her stay at my place for a while until she found one. It's interesting how I had no problem offering up my home to her yet I had so much trouble doing that with Rae. Mary politely declined. Her work was paying for her move and she didn't want to impose on me.

After we finished dinner, I paid our bill and walked her to her car. She politely gave me a friend zone hug and a kiss on the cheek.

Oh, well, I guess.

* * *

The next morning, I woke up with red, itchy eyes. Thinking it was just allergies, I soothed them with over the counter eye drop medication and opted to wear my glasses instead of my contacts. This was my first Saturday alone in my apartment in a long time. It was eerily quiet and cold. Choosing to brush off any regret in my decision to break up with Rae, I turned on the radio and cleaned house. I tossed out all the vegan foods and condiments in my fridge and kitchen cabinets. I pitched the ugly orange plates that Rae's best friend Olivia had given "us" to use and the newspapers Rae requested I subscribe to for her to read on weekends she was at my place.

"I can't miss my horoscopes," she had argued.

By late afternoon, I was tired and ready for a nap. Dramatically dropping myself on my couch, the scent of lavender and lemon met my nose and my heart rate slightly increased. Her scent still lingered on my couch pillows she insisted we have when I bought my new furniture. Tossing them onto the floor, I turned on my television and began to watch a movie. My blurry vision returned instantly during the movie. Frustrated, I turned off the TV. I laid back on my couch and closed my eyes.

I awoke to the sound of my cell phone ringing.

"Hello?"

"You want to go to a club tonight?" It was Mary.

Eyes squinting, I glanced at my phone to see what time it was. 9:35 P.M.

I slept for 7 hours?!

"Leo? Helloooo?" Mary sounded tipsy and a bit too loud for my groggy brain.

"Uh...yeah, sorry. I was napping."

"Napping?!" she giggled. "Well, wake up and go to a club with me! The hotel bar cut me off." Except when Mary spoke it slurred and sounded more like *Da hotel bah cuhmeoff.*

Shaking my head, I smiled and said, "Tell you what, Mary. I'll come pick you up and we'll go to a club so you can sweat out some of that vodka and cranberry juice on the dance floor."

"HELL YEAH!" she exclaimed.

Wincing at her yelling, I said, "I'll be there in twenty."

Once I was at the hotel, I had the front desk ring Mary's room. The aesthetic of the hotel was 80's orange retro furniture and the receptionist looked old enough to be the hotel's very first employee.

"Hello, we have a gentleman here to pick you up...um, what? I-I-I'm sorry ma'am I can't really understand you...I see, yes, I will," the receptionist said calmly. After hanging up the phone she looked at me and said, "She is on her way down."

After a good fifteen minutes, I was about to ask the receptionist what Mary's room number was so I could check on her when I heard Mary yell across the lobby from the elevators.

"Hey, you!" she yelled.

I took a moment to take her in as she walked toward me. She was wearing a tight leopard pattern dress with red heels that had to be at least six inches. Her red hair was curled and her eye make-up seemed to be smudged. Her eyes were heavy, like she could fall asleep at any moment.

"You look so hot right now," Mary breathed seductively as she came uncomfortably close to me. Her breath was a mixture of alcohol and cigarettes.

Avoiding eye contact, I gently pushed her away from me and said, "You look great, too, Mary. Are you sure you're good to go out?"

Mary jerked her head back dramatically and loudly proclaimed, "Buzz kill! I'm just fine! Plus, I want to dance like you said! Sweat this shit out!" She clapped her hands. "Let's go!"

Clearing my throat, I smiled and said, "Sure, let's go. But no more drinks for you. Just dancing. Deal?"

Mary attempted to stand up straight and saluted me. "Deal, Officer Leo." She broke out in hysterical laughter and stumbled. It reminded me of a joke I saw online that compared women in heels to baby giraffes learning to walk. Giggling at the thought, I helped her walk out of the hotel lobby.

* * *

My eyes had started to burn again on the way to the only decent club in town, Pacific Blue. I was quickly putting eye drops in my eyes by the bar when Mary grabbed my arm and caused me to drop the bottle on the floor.

"Dance with me!" she pleaded loudly. A new song had just come on over the speakers.

"Damn it! My eye drops," I said, not loud enough for her to hear.

The music and dark lighting caused sensory overload while my eyes continued to water. I had finally found the bottle a few feet away and, while squinting my eyes, watched in annoyance as two college guys heading towards the bar stepped on the bottle.

"Come on, Leo. Dance with me! This is my *favorite* song!" Mary was shaking her hips and had both my biceps in each hand.

Then, as if on cue, I smelled lavender and lemon. I let out a quick gasp as my eyes began to tear up like I was cutting a big, red onion. I pushed myself away from her and swiftly took off my glasses to put the palms of my hands over my eyes. I started to bend over slightly when I vaguely heard Mary speak. I couldn't make out the words she was saying over the bass of the song and the pain controlling my eyes.

Blinking excessively and rubbing my eyes with my fingers I finally heard Mary shout, "What's wrong?"

"I don't know," I shouted back.

She took my hand and lead me down to the basement floor where the bathrooms were. I could smell a smoking lounge close by, except the smell wasn't tobacco. The music from upstairs had muffled to a loud, repetitive bass vibration. My eyes were so blurry, even with my glasses still on, I could barely see her features clearly.

"What's wrong, Leo? Did you get something your eyes? They're really, really red." Mary's demeanor had changed. She had sobered up quite a bit.

Just as I was about to explain to Mary the pink eye symptoms I had earlier, a woman with two other blondes walked past.

"Leo? Hey!" Olivia touched my shoulder. I recognized her nasally voice instantly.

"Olivia? Hey." My tone was intentionally flat. The last thing I wanted to deal with right now on this failed night out with Mary was my ex-girlfriend's best friend.

"Are you alright, man? Your eyes look really bad," Olivia questioned.

"He doesn't know what's wrong," Mary responded for me. "I think we should just leave." I could hear Mary lighting a cigarette.

"But I drove and you definitely can't drive, I don't care what you say," I argued as I tried to squint and get a better view of Mary's face to read her expression.

"Well, my friends and I are leaving right now. I can call an Uber for you guys if you want." I glanced in Olivia's direction and saw her take out her cell phone. I heard the tapping of her nails on the touch screen. "There. I have an Uber coming for us and one for you guys."

"Thanks so much," Mary said as I felt her hand gently rub my back in a comforting fashion.

I couldn't read Olivia's face, but her tone told me everything I needed to know when she asked, "So how is Rae doing?"

I felt Mary's hand immediately abandon my back.

"I'm not really sure. I broke up with her on Wednesday night," I tried to casually reply, ignoring the throbbing pain in my eyes.

"Wait. You broke up with her?" she questioned.

"Yeah. It was just time—"

"Did your eyes start hurting after the break up?" Olivia interrupted.

Not understanding her point, I said, "Yeah. So?"

Olivia was silent for a moment, just long enough that I felt everything around me pause. "You know Rae is heavy into rituals and magic and shit, right?"

I chuckled and instantly brushed off her suspicions, "Rae is a tarot card reader. Hardly a voodoo queen." I put my hands in my pockets and felt Mary's hand on my back, rubbing it gently.

Olivia was silent again.

"What? You think Rae cursed me or something because I broke up with her? That's a bit dramatic," I mocked.

Olivia remained silent for what felt like hours until a notification on her phone chimed. "Our Ubers are here," she announced.

* * *

That night I had a dream. I felt my body floating, like I was in water. I was in a dining room; one I had never seen before. It had a large oak dining table with eight tall, oak chairs. Sitting at the end of the table was Rae. She was dressed in a white satin gown that had a long train pooled around her bare feet on the floor. Her hair seemed much longer; it was almost reaching the floor. The entire table was covered with white candles of all different sizes. They were glowing through the mist of the room, inviting me to come closer, but I did not move. I couldn't move. It was like I was watching an old home movie of someone else's memories.

Rae held a black candle that sat in front of her and scribbled weird symbols into it. She lit the candle, closed her eyes and lifted her hands close to it, like she was using it to warm up. I felt goosebumps over my entire body. I tried to scream, yet my lips stayed sealed.

Rae abruptly opened her eyes and began to speak, "Andromalius, ruler of legions, punisher of thieves and wickedness. Andromalius, I, with the power of my mind, summon you on this full moon night."

Full moon night? The last full moon was Wednesday when I...broke up with Rae.

There was a cold, dead silence. Suddenly, a sharp wind rushed through the room and caused every white candle flame to extinguish. All that remained lit was the black candle sitting in front of Rae. I tried to move again. I wanted out of this dream so badly. I had never seen this side of Rae's spiritualistic crap before. I still could not move. It was as if I had to be here, watching this.

Rae took a deep breath in and tilted her head to the ceiling. She closed her eyes and spoke again, her voice sounding foreign and deep. "Andromalius, a man I loved stole a piece of my heart. I demand your strength and help in gaining it back." She continued to whisper softly now towards the ceiling, eyes still closed.

"I feel your strength and accept it," she announced and outstretched her arms. "Next, I demand you grant my spell to punish this man."

I began to close my eyes, begging for this crazy bitch's charade to be over and for me to wake up in my nice, warm bed. A loud growl attacked my eardrums and I instantly opened my eyes. Rae was now standing, arms hanging at her sides. Her head hung down, facing the ground, her black hair covering most of her face.

I could hear her softly reciting, "By my might, by all that is right, curse Leo Hamilton and take away his sight." She continued to say this a few more times until faintly, I heard our song playing somewhere in the distance.

I felt instant nausea. The song grew in volume and began to echo throughout the misty room as Rae continued to stand like a statue with her head hung and her hair covering her face.
As the chorus of the song began to play, Rae robotically lifted her face and her black eyes looked directly at me. She sang the chorus so deep and raspy that I began to think she wasn't even Rae anymore. Alarmed, I panicked and swung my arms in a backstroke, barely moving away from the scene in front of me when everything went black. I couldn't hear or see anything.

Then I was awake.

I laid in my bed, sweat pooling around my entire pillow case and my back. I sat up and blinked excessively, struggling to see in my dark bedroom. I could finally make out my dresser, my closet door, my bed, and eventually my entire room.

My heart still racing, I ran into my bathroom and vomited. I climbed back into bed and fell back asleep as if the dream had never even happened.

* * *

A week later, I sat patiently in the waiting room of Dr. Justin Vorhees, the local eye specialist. Since my dream that night, my eyesight had grown exponentially worse. I had gone completely blind in my right eye, with my left eye not too far behind. I was desperate for a cure and was beginning to fear Olivia's ridiculous idea was true.

The sterile smelling waiting room had walls that were white, which I was happy I could still see. I sat alone in the waiting room, anxiously awaiting my fate when I heard a song begin to play on the small, black radio next to the receptionist.

I shut my eyes immediately, trying to block out the song. Instead, the blackness brought me back to that dream, that foreign voice, and all I could see was her face.

I opened my eyes again to stare at the blurry, white walls, breathing deeply in and out of my nose. My knuckles turned white as I intensely gripped the lobby chair armrests.

Make it STOP!

Swiftly, as if by my telepathic request, a short, older nurse opened the waiting room door to rescue me. "Dr. Vorhees will see you now, Leo."

Song of the Dragonborn

By Corinth Panther

The army stood in the field of battle. The six generals watching for any sign of their enemy. Their numbers were huge, easily three hundred thousand as they stood on the field. No opposing force could have more. They'd brought all their men, all their warriors to this spot so they could win. The generals had prepared well for this day. They'd studied the charts, spoken to others who'd faced them and they'd learned all they could about their enemy. Today was the proving day, when their people would face their greatest foe and win.

The soldiers had joked and laughed the night before. Some had taken to drink as though they'd already won the day. Others had bedded down early, preparing in their own way for the coming battle. Their weapons were held tight, they felt ready. Their fellows were with them. No, they could not lose, not when they were so well trained, so prepared for what was about to happen.

A few had remarked that this was a fool's errand. They'd read the same charts, seen the same reports. A few didn't think they could win, but the generals said they could, so here the men stood, ready to do battle and take home the victory where no others could.

From a distance, they heard chanting in a language no one understood slowly getting closer with what sounded like drums. As the sound got nearer, the army came to realize the drums were pounding feet, marking time. The sound grew, the voices became clear. The words still weren't understood but no one needed to know what they sang to feel a chill run up their spines. The men shifted uneasily, the generals looked at each other. They could lose their army if they couldn't settle the men.

One of them yelled "Steady!" but the sound drowned them out.

Their own drums began trying to outdo the approaching army. They needed to boost morale now more than ever. There was something about the chant, something haunting about the words, though none could understand them. The leader shouted for the men to sing. He wanted to drown out the sound, to show how much bigger his army was and try to intimidate the opposing side.

As if on cue another set of voices seemed to echo the first, drowning the standing army out. The sound filled the air rolling over them, bouncing off anything it could. As though magic worked, the chant grew, and some men covered their ears, trying to recall the words to their own song. Others didn't open their mouths but listened, taking comfort in the words. A few lowered their weapons, ready to give up without a fight.

"Sir, I think they just keep repeating it," a lesser general told one of the higher ups. Others around them had stopped singing and the drummers had stilled their beats, unable to keep their own rhythm.

"What are they saying?" another demanded. He'd been informed--nay, told--they couldn't mass more than half his own numbers. While the opposing army wasn't yet in view he knew his information had been wrong. No way half his numbers could produce that volume. If he lived to see this battle end, he'd find out why someone had lied, and then see them hung for their misinformation.

Coming over a small rise, the first of the lines crested the horizon, riding down until the first ten lines could be seen before stopped. The forward warriors rode huge cats, or at least they looked like cats. Many of the next rank were feline looking, walking on two legs. Others looked to be humanoid. They were all marking time, pounding their feet on the ground. Even this far away the army could feel it, the way the ground shook with each beat.

Before the generals could think, the sound vanished. The feet stilled, though the chanting continued. The three generals who had been convinced they could win watched the sight, feeling their men becoming demoralized. Their numbers were huge, far more than his spies, the charts, or even the survivors told him. They'd been misled. Those few who'd spoken out and stated this was a fool's dream had been right. Oh how they all wished they'd listened now, and fell back rather than marching forward.

"Sir, I know what they're saying," a young boy no older than ten announced.

The general looked at him. He was one of the sword carriers for the horsemen. His job was to stay well back when the fighting began. Most of the children here had a job: some cared for the horses, others handled the cooking. It was a way to prevent families from breaking up.

"What?" he asked, not sure he wanted to believe a child in this matter.

"We come to fight, we come to die. We keep this land, we shall not fall. We stand for all, we stand for none. We shall fight, we shall die. We keep this land. None shall fall. We come to win, we come to live." The boy's eyes were transfixed on the army standing before them. "We are the Feline, none shall forget."

When the boy finished his translation the chanting stopped. Nothing moved. The cats and their riders stood perfectly still. The generals looked at each other, not so much as an ear twitched or a tail swayed. The cats had to be the most disciplined animals ever. Even their own mounts shifted, flicked an ear or swatted a fly. The six generals gathered were in awe of their enemy. No matter what happened today, they would always recall this moment. The sheer numbers before them, the sound and the way nothing stirred.

A moment passed, then another. The men gripped their weapons, ready to for the charge. A sole figure broke from the front line; a woman, they noted, without helmet or armor. She wore brown leather, loose and easy to move in, a sword strapped to her back. The cat she rode was pure black, tall enough to be a large pony. It moved with ease three paces. No one moved to close the hole in their ranks. The generals snickered to themselves, spotting the golden hilt. An ornate weapon wasn't good for more than show and flash. This woman had no business on the field of battle.

She turned the massive cat to the right, then slowly trotted down the line. "Today we came to the field of battle as the challenged. They have heard our chant and have not run. They are brave--foolish--but brave. We shall honor them in death as they have honored us in life. We stand, my friends, here to defend the world we call home." She reached the end of the line, turned, and trotted back the way she'd come. "They will fall before our claws and our teeth, but not before they learn never to mess with us again. We have no fear of death, we shall stand as long as one of their numbers remain. We shall not fall in vain." She reached the halfway mark.

"We ride today in glory and for peace. We shall end these foes and hold our lands. If there are any who refuse to fight, break the ranks now. No dishonor will come to you or your kind." She reached the far end, turning her mount once more and watched her people. None broke away. She knew they wouldn't. Her people were warriors. They wouldn't turn tail no matter the numbers they faced.

Every word she'd spoken was in the language of her enemy. They could hear her, and understood what she said. Would they break away, flee as they should? Slowly she walked her cat back to the spot she'd left. None were moving on the other side either. Good. She'd been looking forward to a real battle for some time. When she reached the location she'd left, she turned her mount forward.

"Then—" She drew her sword over her head, crystal, reflecting the sunlight in rainbow patterns and razor sharp.

The rest of her line followed pulling swords, daggers, staves, bows and other weapons the generals couldn't name. The generals thought they saw the flash of white near the ground where claws were extended. The cats opened their mouths showing off their perfect white teeth. Their own men shook, ready to break.

"Steady," the generals called out. "This is just a scare tactic." At least they all hoped the cats weren't really going to fight. If those cats fought as well, they'd be out numbered three to one.

"We are the Feline!" The chant started up once more, this time in the common tongue. "We came to fight, none shall stand against our might, we shall die but not before they fall. We are the Feline, we come to..." Slowly the crystal sword which she'd held over her head dropped as the last word was uttered from her lips only. "Win."

A roar filled the now-quiet space as the lines rushed forward. The leader fell in when the front line was beside her. Her sword was pulled back, ready to strike. The generals realized they'd been wrong twice over. While the sword looked ornate, it was as functional as their own.

Their leader fought on the front lines. "They have my respect," one barked as he took his helmet. "Charge!" His voice rang out as the cats moved forward nearly silently.

The two armies clashed and the generals knew they were in trouble. In one quick attack over half of his first line fell. From his post on the top of a rise he could see his men fall. They couldn't take even a single one of the mounted riders down. He jerked his head around. Screams rang out as more men fell close at hand. His own archers, who had been trying to give cover to his men, were falling. His eyes followed the line of arrows back. Their archers had more marksmen than his own. These warriors didn't use shields yet they seemed able to avoid the rain of arrows their own men launched.

"Damn it," one of the older generals yelled turning his mount, ready to charge down there himself.

He could hear the clang of metal striking metal. He could smell the metallic scent of blood heavy in the air. He watched as good, well trained men fell to teeth and claws, as well as blades. Those who looked more like cats on two legs held no weapons, not that they needed a weapon; they had claws and teeth just like their four-legged cousins.

It was hard to tell if their men had taken any of the Feline down. One thing was for sure: This was a losing battle. His ass hurt from sitting in the saddle. He glanced at the sun through the cloud of insects which already started to gather. An hour had passed since they'd arrived, so sure they could win. A flock of crows and ravens coming to feast joined the carnage. He felt rather then saw some of his men break away. The chanting did its part, watching their comrades fall so easily did the rest.

The head general looked to his fellows, they nodded. It was time. He raised his horn to his lips and began to blow. Their men fell back. The Feline rushed after the retreating men, driving them back farther, taking more of the men out even as they tried to run. Finally the general could see the leader on the ground, her left arm shredded and bleeding, her mount close by.

As his men fell back behind him, she laughed a wicked sound. "Have you had enough?" Her voice carried so well on the open field before him.

"I see no point in losing more men!" he yelled back.

"Submit we have won today. Leave this place and never challenge us again. Do this and you can leave with those who still live. If you refuse, we shall hunt you down and kill the rest of those men who now shake behind you. You have tasted our strength, generals. Do you wish to see it in full?" Her voice so strong, he wasn't sure she was really as hurt as she seemed.

He looked at his men. No one seemed ready to meet this army again. Sure, he could raise more men but not quickly enough. He looked at the others and they all agreed. This was pointless. To return would be foolish.

"We agree, and we shall spread word of your strength so none are as foolish as we were. Does this please you?"

She nodded. "Yes. It seems you are wise after all. Begone." She swung onto her mount, turning it around. Those of her people who were still on their feet turned as well, chanting anew.

He looked to the boy who had managed to flee the battle. "Now what do they say?"

"We have gone and they have fled. Our strength is great, none shall stand. Leave and live, come and die. None shall stand, we are the Feline, we have won." The chant continued until they were well out of sight and hearing.

The general looked at his men, then at the other leaders beside him. "We shall go and collect our men, then bury them. I also want to know how many they lost."

They all nodded and the slow march to collect the fallen began. When it was all said and done, over half of his men had fallen with close to a hundred of hers. He looked over the battlefield soaked in blood and mud as the camp fires danced as though trying to add a bit of cheer. He could just make out a few cats standing watching them.

"They're keeping an eye on us," one of the generals remarked.

The man nodded. "I can see that." He turned his back to the hill the cats stood on then called out to the men. "We shall camp here for the night then return home." He knew this battle would never be forgotten. His men fought bravely, dying in vain. They'd saved as many of them as they could. Those who died would be remembered and never again would he believe a spy. If he ever got his hands on that fool again he'd wring his neck for this.

In the morning, as they packed at first light and started moving off, he saw the cats turn and leave. It would take time, but they moved as quickly as they could. This land wasn't worth dying over. There were other places for he and his men to go. He glanced at the boy, who looked back at the cat and waved. The cat inclined its head then sat down as though waiting for the boy.

Well, at least most of them would leave, the general thought as he rode his army off the field of battle.

Ghosts

By Alexis Parlier

I stuff my last favorite sweatshirt into my backpack, zip it up, and fling it around my shoulder. My duffel bag is also packed full. I take one last look around my childhood bedroom. Part of me wants to sink to the floor and cry while part of me wants to grab a baseball bat and smash everything to pieces. But the biggest part of me knows that leaving is the only choice I can make right now. I have to get out.

"Ayla, you can't just leave." Mom is pleading with her hands, begging me to stay.

"Just don't. I don't want to hear another lie." I let the anger drip freely.

"Ayla please. You can't just run off with Mason, that's not how this goes. I'm your mother." She tries her stern voice, but it doesn't make my blood turn icy with fear like it might have before. The last thing she could do is ground me right now. Not after I found out what she did.

"Watch me." I slam the front door behind me, letting the bang of wood crashing into wood echo in my head.

Mason's car sits in the front of my driveway, the afternoon sun shining on the black paint while dust settles halfway up the doors. He lives on a dirt road. It's pointless to ever wash it because it'll just get dirty the next day.

His windows are rolled down and soft music lingers out. I see his face and it's enough to give me the strength I need to leave. I look to the backseat that has two backpacks full of his things and a big blue cooler in the middle, containing our food for the next 35 hours. I look to the front seat. Mason is smiling. I feel comfort settle into my bones.

But I'm broken from that feeling by the creaking of my front door behind me and the sounds of my Mom crying behind me.

"Ayla," she croaks.

And I almost turn around, wrap her in my arms, tell her everything will be okay. Just like I always have. Ever since Dad died.

Until I remember, Dad never died. It was all a lie. He left us. Years ago, when I was six.

He left us because she cheated. All of these years I thought my father was dead, when in reality he was just avoiding my mom. Avoiding me. And the pain strikes so deep.

I step off of our minty green porch. I remember painting it with mom when I was 10 years old. We'd laughed for hours after I had accidentally spilled half a can over Mom's feet. The paint had sunk so deep in her toenails that it took a whole week to get it out. The memory almost makes me stay. The pain in my chest resonates through my whole body.

I open Mason's door, throwing my bags next to his. The smell of him is like a thick blanket in the middle of winter, comforting in every way.

"Hi." His voice is warm butter.

I climb into the front seat and sigh loudly, letting my head hit the back of the seat. "Just drive," I whisper. He puts the car into drive, then reaches over and sets his hand gently on my knee.

Before he turns right off of my street, I take a moment to turn around, looking back at my childhood home.

It's painted a salty popcorn color, with shutters white as they can be after years of wear and tear. All the memories flood into me as we turn the corner: memories of me growing up, memories of me living my life, memories that are now darkened with the question of which parts were real. What was a lie? When did she tell the truth?

I shake my head, trying to get out all of the thoughts, trying to ignore the tears threatening to creep into my eyes.

"Are you okay?" Mason is gentle, clutching my knee a little tighter.

"I will be when we get there."

* * *

We're almost out of Illinois as the sun begins to set. It's a beautiful, midwestern early summer night. The humidity is low, but high enough to take away some of the late night chill. I've always felt like there is some sort of magic in a sunset, almost like little whispers of gold are falling from the sky. It hits all of the surfaces, reflecting off of Mason's shiny black hair. It's at the length I love right now; not too long, not too short, but just so.

He looks over to me and smiles.

"What are you staring at weirdo?" He grins.

"You're beautiful, you know that?" Sincerity leaks through my pores as I revel in his subtle beauty. Deep sunlight absorbs in his skin and I swear he's glowing. His teeth are so white against his skin as he smiles at me. My heart is beating slowly, contentedly, as his love coats my body.

"*You're* beautiful." He reaches over and grazes his thumb on my cheek as a tear falls into his thumb, a tear that I didn't know had even fallen.

"Thank you for doing this for me. I'm glad your parents are okay with this. And I'm glad that they're paying for this. I am so thankful for all that everyone is doing for me." I feel a sob escape my chest.

Mason pulls over, pulling me on his lap as we sit on the side of the highway. Cars speed past us as we sit here, me crying into Mason's chest and the sun setting around us. Part of me feels like the crying will never stop, that the gaping hole in my chest where the idea of who my mother was used to fill.

"I'm right here. I'll always be right here," Mason whispers in my ear.

I count to ten in my head, trying to calm myself down. I can feel him staring at me and my breathing starts to even out. I look up to Mason, meeting his deep brown eyes with my hazel ones.

"Thank you." My chin starts to wobble again.

"Shhh, Ayla, it'll be okay." He hugs me tighter. I put my hands to his chest, pushing him away slightly. I wipe away the tears on my face and look at Mason's shirt, which is damp now.

"Your shirt, I really did a number on it." I smile, trying to lighten the mood and distract my thoughts so I don't cry again.

"It's okay, I brought some more." He points to the backseat where our bags lay beside the cooler I forgot about.

"We should probably find somewhere to eat, then we can switch so I can drive for a while." I feel the emptiness in my stomach from not eating all day.

"Sounds good." He moves back in front of the steering wheel, putting his seat back in place and starts to move the gear into drive.

"Wait!" I burst out.

"Wha—"

I cut him off with a kiss. I try putting all of my thanks, all of my love, all of my excitement of getting away from home for a little while into this kiss. I feel Mason push his hands through my long ashy hair. Butterflies flutter deep in my stomach, something that hasn't gone away even after a year of dating.

He starts to pull away and I try bringing him back in, but he's persistent. "You need to eat, Ayla. We have all the time in the world for kissing. And we have to get going if we're going to get to California in a couple days," he reminds me, pulling me back to the present, back to the goal at hand.

"You're right, let's go." We buckle our seatbelts and Mason merges back onto the highway. I grab the cooler from the backseat, curious to see what treasure lies within.

* * *

After we eat, I take the driver's seat. Leading us out of Illinois and into Iowa. It's dark now, nighttime has settled around us like a cool blanket.

Mason faded into a deep slumber about 20 minutes ago. He doesn't snore, something I've always been grateful for. Even though we just graduated high school a couple weeks ago, we've spent the night together a few times. Our parents had no idea and they probably still don't.

Music plays softly in the background and my window is cracked. The summer night is so calm, it almost makes me sleepy. But then I remember where we are headed. Across country. To California, the Golden State. I've never seen the ocean, and although it terrifies me, I'm so excited to see the beach and feel the sun on my shoulders.

Also, my dad is there.

The father I thought had been dead for 12 years, the father who left me when my mom made a mistake. The father I had shoved aside in my head to help with my mother's grief over his presumed death. My anger towards them is equal. A father who ran away from me and a mother who lied to me my whole life. It made me numb almost, all of this anger appearing seemingly overnight. I guess what surprises me most is that my mom hid it for so long, and did so successfully.

But she wasn't expecting her sister, Tabitha, to come into town last week.

I had never met Mom's little sister. She always told me, "Tabby is reckless. She does what she wants. She's never been one to stay around for family, even when Grammy and Grandpapi were still alive." Or little tales like that. Except now I know the truth. She was staying away because my mom was lying to me and everyone around her.

I had always thought that me and Mom moved so suddenly when I was younger because she couldn't stand to be in the same town that she grew up in, the same town that Dad had died in. I always thought that she never kept in contact with anyone from her hometown because it was hard to be known as a widow, a single mother.

My Aunt Tabitha threw my life in a spiral when she came to our house one night, banging on the door, screaming at Mom. Yelling that it had taken years of silence from her sister to finally say enough is enough. To stop lying to everyone. To stop lying to me.

I remember how white my mom's face had gotten as she sat on the couch, staring off towards the wall. My mouth was agape. All the blood left my face and a chill spread across my body as if someone had dunked me into a pool full of ice.

I let Tabitha in, with all her rage and all of her disbelief. She stared at the both of us. Each of us in shock. Mom because she got caught, me because I realized I had been mourning a father who was still alive and well. I remember Tabitha sitting next to me, asking if I was okay, if I needed any further explanation. I made her promise to tell me more when I came back.

Then I drove to Mason. Numb and confused. I don't remember how I got to his house, but when I showed up, he was so concerned that I wouldn't talk. Instead, I remember collapsing into his arms as sobs rocked my entire body.

He went with me the next day to talk to my Aunt Tabby at a coffee shop in town. She told us everything. Answered all of my questions. Apologized that she let it happen for so long and that she didn't try sooner to make my mom come to terms with what she had done. She offered for me to stay with her in Chicago until I went to college. I told her I would call her once I decided.

I texted her about this trip a few days ago, once everything was worked out with Mason's parents. She said she supported me, that it was healthy for me, and that she would be there if I needed anything.

The numbness starts to creep back into the forefront of my mind as I drive down the dark highway. Mason sighs in his sleep, so softly I almost don't hear it, but it pulls me out of my head. I smile at him, thinking to myself how lucky I am that he's here with me.

* * *

We're almost all the way through Utah. Mason has been driving for ten hours, only stretching for five minute intervals at a time. We haven't talked much. Most of the time we're singing along to the radio or just enjoying the drive. He's giving me the space I need, not trying to pry into my mind, and I love him so much for it.

"Do you remember the first date we went on?" I look over to his face. He's smiling softly, his eyes are on the road, but he's staring into the past.

"Of course. How could I forget it? You were so shy, you barely made eye contact with me." I smile at the memory. He had asked me out in school and ran away after I said yes. It was so weird, but so charming at the same time.

"That's because you looked breathtaking in that sundress." His voice is gravelly.

"That was on purpose." I reach over and pinch his arm lightly.

"And what did you expect me to talk to you about while we sat in the drive-in movie? I was focused on the plot." He glances over and winks at me.

I smile, letting the memory float around me. Whenever I watched *The Notebook* before I met Mason, I always thought their summer romance and instant connection was fake. I always thought there was no way people just fell in love so quickly. But then Mason came along.

He reaches over and grabs my hand as he continues to stare at the road ahead. Just like he did on our first date. Not making eye contact, but this time his smile is lighting up his entire face.

"I can't believe I just grabbed your hand like that on a first date. I am weird, you're right."

I laugh, gripping his hand even tighter. "It's okay, I love you anyway." Happy tears swell in my eyes.

"I love you too, Ayls." He lifts his hand to my cheek and pinches it softly.

When we first get to California, I'm bummed that it all looks so normal, but as we near the coast, I can feel the air almost clear up, as if the ocean is blowing away any impurities. The air feels light, and I feel like I can smell the salt.

I can also feel the anxiety blossom in my stomach as the thought of meeting my dad goes to the forefront of my mind.

"I'm so ready for this hotel tonight. I have missed sleeping in a bed and taking a shower." He scrunches his nose.

"I have also missed sleeping in a bed. My neck is so sore from my head lolling side to side when I sleep." I rub the back of my neck at the thought.

"But first, we're hitting the beach." He taps his fingers against the steering wheel excitedly. I smile, but don't say anything back. I'm too anxious, as we get closer and closer to the coastline, heading towards the seagulls and seafoam.

The closer we get, the greener and bluer everything seems to get. Green is everywhere, but the blue sky seems enormous, holding small white, fluffy clouds that drift slowly in the sky. The salt in the air is now more defining, I can feel it settling softly onto my skin.

And suddenly, it's there.

It's everywhere, the ocean. The size of it is almost unsettling, making me feel small compared to its massive pool of water. Except the beauty takes away any unsettling feeling that began to rise in my chest. Sunshine glitters off of the surface of the water, sparkling so much that I almost want to put my sunglasses back on.

"Wow," Mason breathes beside me.

"I couldn't have said it better myself," I whisper back. He reaches over and turns the radio off. He rolls the windows down the rest of the way, letting the full ocean breeze enter the car. Salt air invades my lungs, captivating all of my senses. It's almost as if I can reach into the air and pick out tiny morsels of salt. I never thought it was like this, I never thought the ocean could bring this many sensations to your body without even needing to enter it. I'm mesmerized.

Mason puts the car in park. He looks over at me with a grin on his face. There lies so much excitement in his eyes that I completely forget why I'm really here. Instead, I open my door and start grabbing our things. He, of course, packed the essentials: beach towels, coconut sunscreen, water bottles, and all of the snacks that are still in the cooler. We grab them all, smiling as we do so, and he starts to leap down the stairs two at a time towards the beach. I follow him, laughing silently until we hit the sand.

I take off my flip flops and feel goosebumps rise across my skin at the coolness of it all. I stare down at my toes as sand fills each crevice. I look up to ask Mason where we should set up but he's already gone and in the water. I make my way towards him, noticing all of the people who are spread out along the beach. Teenagers are bumping a volleyball back and forth while small children make sandcastles with buckets. Adults are in various positions, lounging on their towels or yelling at their kids to not go so deep in the water.

I feel my breath halt in my lungs as I hit the first patch of hot sand. I almost want to put my shoes back on, but after a few seconds the warmth becomes soothing on the bottoms of my feet. I changed into my best bathing suit when we stopped at a rest stop on the way here and I'm already excited for the tan I'll get today.

"Ayla!" Mason shouts my name, waving me towards him and the water.

I find where Mason put some of our things and set the rest down. I look back up to find Mason thigh-deep in the ocean. He looks so at peace in the water. His olive skin absorbs the sun reflecting off of the water and his smile is almost as bright as the sun itself.

He's smirking at me, holding his arms open to me, asking me to come to him with his eyes. I take off towards him, squealing as the cold water hits my toes and Mason picks me up, twirling me around. He sets me down in the water, which rests at my waist. I look out on the water. It looks as if it will never end. The vastness of it is extraordinary and it takes my breath away. I feel so small, but so connected at the same time. Water seeps into my skin, sun warms my shoulders, and Mason is holding my hand. Right now, I feel like I have the whole world at my fingertips. Right now, it feels like maybe my whole life hadn't been crashing down on me for over a week.

And right now, those thoughts are drowned out by the beauty that caresses me.

* * *

Mason has his arms wrapped around me as the sun dips into the water. The sunset hues make this scene magical. People have left the beach, going back to their homes after a long, tiring day in the sun, so it's fairly quiet and beyond peaceful.

My head moves slowly with Mason's breathing. The rhythm is lulling me to sleep with the soft sound of the waves hitting the sand and the warmth on my skin from getting a tad bit too much sun. I feel my eyes start to close.

"Despite every reason why we're here, this trip has already been worth it." Mason's voice flicks away the sleep trying to overtake my body. I agree with him by nodding my head against his shoulder. This is the first time he's brought up the reason why we're here all day and part of me wishes he would just let us enjoy this sunset in peace.

"I've really been giving you your space with all that's been going on Ayls, but I need to say something and I don't want to upset you, so just listen okay?" So much softness resonates in his voice that I can't find it in myself to be mad at him for wanting to talk.

"Okay," I whisper, keeping my eyes on the water in front of me.

"I just want you to remember that it's okay if you still love her. It's okay to find the courage and strength inside of yourself to forgive her, Ayla. She made a huge mistake. Two huge mistakes. I think it's been too hard for her to admit to herself that she needs to face up for what she did. She is still your mother, no matter what she does, no matter the mistakes she has made. I'm not trying to downgrade how you feel, and I'm not saying you don't have a right to be angry with her, but just know that one day you need to find it within yourself to forgive her. Not for her, but for you. I can't stand to watch this eat you alive. I can see how bad it's bothering you, and for a good reason, but I just want to see you happy. I love you so much Ayla. It kills me that I can't fix any of this for you." His breath is soft but strong.

Tears roll down my cheek, silently, slowly. I can feel Mason's fingers lightly brushing up and down my arm. He's so supportive that I can't let the tears stop chasing each other.

"I love you Mason," I whimper.

He pulls me onto his chest for the second time today and lets me cry into his shirt.

The words he said were entirely true, but they create a wide set of mixed emotions. I want to feel the peace that he's explaining, but the anger is too strong. It's dragging me down, like a weight yanking my heart into the pit of my stomach.

But she's my mother. And right now, that's not enough to evaporate all of the anger; but eventually I think I will get there.

Mason is so patient, so kind, showing me the support I desperately need. Giving me the advice that I'm too blind to face myself.

He kisses the top of my head. And after a few minutes my tears stop their wild goose chase towards each other. I lift my head off of Mason's chest and plant a soft kiss on his lips. He smiles beneath it.

"Can we come back tomorrow?" I smile at him.

"Of course."

* * *

I wake up with the rattling of the air conditioner and the thought that today I'm going to meet my father. The man who I thought has been dead my entire life. A man who hasn't taken time to get to know me at all.

And maybe I should've told him I was coming, but after all these years, I don't think that applies anymore. I never got the heads up that my dad had left me my whole life.

I've only seen one picture of him my entire life. It always haunted me, like a ghost. I feel cold just trying to imagine his face, and a shiver travels through my body.

Mason is still in a deep slumber beside me, his face is open and vulnerable. I've always loved watching him sleep. He looks so peaceful. I hate to wake him. I drug him all the way out here, driving straight here with breaks only short enough to get the kinks out of his neck. He needs this sleep, and I need to prepare myself for today.

I slip out of the bed slowly and softly, trying not to move the bed even an inch. The bed is dense and cushiony, which makes my silent escape even easier. I tiptoe to the bathroom, slowly closing the door. I make a sigh of relief when it closes with the softest click.

The bathtub is lined with mini bottles of soap and folded white fluffy towels. I turn the shower on full blast, letting it heat up and fog the mirror as I stare at my reflection.

Which parts of my face do I harness from my father? My hazel eyes, high cheekbones, arched eyebrows, slightly round nose, or freckles on my cheeks that only come out when it's summer? Or will I only look at him and see a stranger?

My heart contracts as anxiety shoots through my veins. It almost feels like a thick black sludge weighing my veins down whilst sending panic to every nerve in my brain. I almost feel like I'm going to be sick, but I step into the shower instead. I let the heat within the water wash away some of the panic.

I'm almost finished with my shower, letting the last of the conditioner run out of my hair and down the drain, when Mason knocks on the door.

"Are you going to save any hot water?" he jokes through the door.

"That's not how hotels work, Mace." I feel a grin stretch out my cheeks.

"Well I'm bored, so hurry up."

I smile, turning off the knobs and wrapping myself in a towel.

I step back in front of the mirror. The steam has covered it completely, and now I see none of myself. Instead I'm just a blur, but it gives me comfort, reminding me that I'm not who I look like. Instead, I'm just who I am inside.

* * *

We spend the afternoon lounging on the beach, with the occasional dip in the ocean. The seagulls are louder today, or maybe it's just something I never noticed yesterday.

The days spent here are filled with so much color. So much joy. So much love. I never want to leave, but I know that what I have to do today is something that is necessary. Even though I am so terrified, I need to meet the other half of who I am. I need to know why my mother thought that she deserved a life without grief even though she sabotaged my life with him. I need to know if he's worth all the destruction in my life.

Mason holds out his hand, offering to lift me up off the sand. His face is hard to read and I'm not sure what he's thinking. But I have too much going on in my own mind to ask.

We walk back to his car, our hands swinging back and forth in the silence.

Once again he's giving me space to think. I watch as he plugs in the address to my father's house into his phone. The fastest route pops up on his phone, but he chooses the one that adds five minutes. I look over to him, thanking him without saying anything.

He gives me a soft smile in return and grabs my hands as we pull out of the parking space.

The drive to my dad's house is filled with nothing but the music in the background and the breeze from the ocean filling the car. I almost want to stick my head out of the window to soak up the rays and to smell the salty air.

It's so beautiful. I can imagine myself living here with my dad in another life, one where maybe I got to choose which parent I wanted to live with, or maybe even if I saw him for weeks at a time. It would be like a vacation, coming here to see him. I feel butterflies flutter in my stomach that maybe after today he will want to see me more.

I push that thought away as I try to keep my mind clear of any expectations I might have. Mason is singing along to the radio, reminding me that whenever he's around me, I will always have my own personal sunshine.

The song on the radio cuts out as the GPS voice comes over the speakers, reminding us our turn is in .5 miles. My breathing is starting to increase and I can feel my pulse start to skyrocket. Mason squeezes my hand.

We make a left turn into a subdivision filled with cookie cutter houses. Children ride their bikes down the streets, dogs bark behind metal fences, and there's a strong smell of barbecue. I try to imagine Mom living in a place like this and the images don't fit. Which makes the anxiety run higher in my brain and stomach. I have nothing in common with this man I'm about to meet.

Nothing except my blood.

I feel like I'm going to be sick as Mason pulls into the driveway. There's no sign of activity, which gives me some hope that maybe I won't have to face this today.

"You can do this Ayls, I believe in you. And I love you. Don't forget that." He pulls my head so I'm forced to look at him. There's so much support in his eyes that it calms me, just enough to make me get out of the car and walk up the porch steps.

I feel numb as I knock on the door. My heart is practically beating out of my chest and my veins feel like they're on fire.

The door opens. And I see my ghost. I see my eyes. My cheekbones. My hair. On a man, a man who happens to be my father. My father who also looks like *he's* just seen a ghost, too.

"Ayla," he whispers in shock.

Right before he slams the door in my face.

The Song the Summer Sang

by Lindsey Sanford

The breeze coming across the water carried with it not only the tinge of the lake, but also the indistinguishable smell of what was to come these next three months. Her fingers already ached with the thought of tying hundreds of friendship bracelets and were sticky with countless unopened Band-Aids. The paper banner flapped gently in the wind, the words WELCOME CAMPERS painted on triangles and hung between two large wooden poles. Rows of kayaks were lined along the bank of the water, nestled safely in the reeds. The rope-swing swayed from the thickest branch of the old oak tree, far enough over the water that kids could launch into the lake below. Bridgette took it all in; reveled in the silence that would be shattered come tomorrow morning.

She had started as a camper at Orange Lagoon Summer Camp at the age of seven. Ten years later, she had earned a coveted spot as a counselor.

She was more than ready. She had made notes, overanalyzed every foreseeable situation. She had her speech prepared for when tearful campers wanted to leave as soon as their mom and dad drove away. She had memorized all the songs and the dance motions that went along with each. She had prepped the entire year leading up to this very summer. Because this was what Bridgette did: She planned. She faltered in the unexpected, lost sense of herself in the unknown.

This summer, she vowed, would be the summer she figured herself out beyond straight A's and marching band.

She was ready for everything this summer would bring.

Everything except him...

The clinking of silverware on champagne flutes catapulted her back to the present. The gilded chandeliers cast lightning bugs around the expansive ballroom. Gowns of silken paper-mâché swept across the dance floor. Waiters moved through the room, switching out glasses of bubbly and clearing away dinner plates.

Bridgette Barlow kept as far from the festivities as she could; attempted to stay hidden behind a group of burly and raucous men. According to the indisputable rules of wedding etiquette, she had seven minutes left of her required half-an-hour before she could slip out unnoticed. There would be no indication she had even been there, save for the shards of her broken heart celebrators would unexpectedly drag home with them, and the gift card she'd dropped into the box on her way in.

"You made it," a voice said from beside her. Her stomach twisted like vines, grew thorns that rivaled those of the centerpiece roses.

Forcing herself to look at him, Bridgette replied, "I did RSVP." She was surprised that what came out was words and not the ugly sob gathering in her throat. Somehow, she'd learned to speak to him over the years instead of stuttering like she had that warm June afternoon ten or so years ago. Her cheeks warmed at how tongue-tied she had been around him in the beginning. But guys like Axel Young weren't apt to talk to girls like Bridgette. Society had long ago taught her the only reason the popular homecoming king approached the chubby, freckled, red-headed band nerd was on a dare from his friends. Unfortunately, Bridgette didn't have a pair of glasses she could take off to instantly make herself ten times hotter.

Axel smiled down at her. It was a look made of cicadas and stolen kisses under summer moons. It was cheap hotel-bar drinks and the rekindling of too many years passed. It was promises of a future another woman had received instead.

"So did thirty-five other people who are definitely not here," he replied.

"Oh no!" Bridgette said with gentle sarcasm. "Don't worry. I'm sure someone here bought the $250.00 silk sheets you registered for." She winked at him before draining her glass of very expensive wine.

"Was it you?" he asked. "With all your bestselling author money?"

"Nope," Bridgette replied. "I got you salt and pepper shakers."

"Ah. They'll go great with the other seven sets we have."

Bridgette shrugged a freckled shoulder. "I hope frogs fit your home decor."

He hated frogs. She had laughed until her sides ached whenever a camper begged Axel to help them catch the toads croaking under the dock. The other female counselors had found his disgust endearing. Then again, Axel Young could have set the camp on fire and they'd have found the gesture romantic.

He laughed, the sound cavernous as it traveled through him. It was the body of the Axel she had kissed goodbye on a busy New York street. It was *not* the one to which she had clung that final afternoon at Orange Lagoon, the smell of sunscreen and citronella thick as sweat on their skin. As the last of the campers piled into cars, tanned hands waving excited farewells, Bridgette had sobbed her own goodbye into Axel's t-shirt. She had never been the girl who preferred romance novels over horror stories. In fact, she had come to camp expecting a Friday the 13th summer. Instead, she had gotten *The Notebook* meets *The Babysitter's Club*. And all the heartache that came with both.

It was the first, and last, summer romance she ever had. Axel had tainted the warmer days for her. So much so, that she had foregone lazy beach days with college friends for wine coolers in an air-conditioned apartment and her memories purged onto the screen of her laptop. While her roommates complained about sunburns, Bridgette breathed life into Illiana and Roman, two characters who fell in love at band camp the summer of their senior year.

It was happenstance, really, a chance encounter with the right person that turned Illiana and Roman's tragic love story into a New York Times best seller. Bridgette lost herself in those two surrogate characters, then found herself once more when they became the catalyst that brought she and Axel back together. Now she had lost him, them, and herself once more, buried under files labeled CRAP and NO ONE WILL READ THIS BOOK.

"Dance with me," Axel said, extending his hand. The light from the chandelier bounced off his shiny new wedding ring. Bridgette blinked and glanced around the ballroom, looking for his bride.

"No," she said, crossing her arms. How was it that after three years she still had to restrain herself to keep from touching him?

When the final note of "The Cupid Shuffle" faded and the first note of the next song began, Bridgette's eyes cut to him. He grinned and wiggled the fingers of his still extended hand. Bridgette sighed, swallowed the memories of him humming this song in her ear, and placed her hand in his. The moment their skin touched, it was like coming home. He led her to the dance floor, then tugged her close. Too close. Achingly and familiarly close.

"Is it purely coincidence that this song happened to come up?" she asked. She rested her free hand on his chest. His heart was a steady drum beneath his pressed white shirt. Her other hand he held aloft waltz-style. They moved in a tiny circle like figures in a jewelry box.

"Of course not," Axel replied. "I requested it." When Bridgette gave him a disgusted look, he hurried to justify his actions. "I could tell you were getting ready to leave. I wanted you to stay for one more song."

Her eyes narrowed and her painted red lips formed a straight line. "You're Still You" by Josh Groban moved their bodies like a puppet master. This song had become the soundtrack to her summer at Orange Lagoon.

They had been at camp for two weeks when Axel's knocking rattled the old door to her cabin. "I think you have company," Bridgette hissed to her bunkmate, Marlee. Mar was the sort of girl Axel would come courting. They would undoubtedly die second in a slasher flick, kabobbed to the bed by a kayak paddle. Marlee had nearly tumbled off the top bunk in a rush to get to the door. She didn't even stop to check herself out in the mirror. *What was that like?* Bridgette wondered. *To walk through this world with that much confidence?*

"It's Axel," Marlee mumbled when she came back into the private sleeping area of the cabin a few seconds later. Her disappointment was a fishing line that yanked Bridgette up so fast she was certain she felt an ab develop.

"And this is bad news?" Bridgette asked, confused. Marlee had been leaving puddles of drool behind whenever she saw Axel. She had also taken to flipping her hair if she so much as sensed him. Bridgette had started to worry about her bunkmate's neck.

"He wants *you*."

Marlee *harrumphed* back into bed and sighed dramatically as she whipped the covers over her body. While Bridgette stewed in her confusion and then her worry, Marlee snipped, "Are you going to go or what?"

This cannot be good, Bridgette thought as she kicked off her blanket and shuffled to the cabin door. *I am definitely being set up for a prank*. The movies Bridgette had watched and the YA books she devoured weekly taught her that nothing good came from this sort of situation.

Bridgette didn't bother to check herself in the mirror, either. She knew what a mess she was; how her pigtails and freckles made her look like Pippi Longstocking. She did, however, tug at her faded t-shirt and fix the cuffs of her ratty sweatpants.

"What?" Bridgette asked apprehensively when she approached the door. Axel stood in the lemon bright glow of the outdoor light. A moth fluttered around it, drawn by the humming. Or maybe, like everyone else, it was drawn to Axel.

The rest of the camp was dark, the nightly bonfire extinguished an hour ago, though wisps of smoke still twisted and curled into the air like garter snakes. Campers were snug as bugs in their own cabins, exhausted from the day's activities. The air was peppered with the lullaby of crickets and the gentle lapping of the lake against the dock. It was the perfect backdrop for someone like Axel. He had the ability to fit into whichever scene he stepped, as if the whole world had been designed for him.

"I can't sleep," Axel said.

"And...?"

He smiled, that boyish, charming grin. "Take a walk with me."

Bridgette pulled away from the door, as if his words were weighted and they'd just slammed into her. "Um..."

"C'mon," he said, cocking his head toward the empty camp. Then he turned and leaped off the small porch. Bridgette knew better. She knew as soon as she stepped outside his friends would dump garbage soup on her head. Her feet, however, did not seem as aware of this as they shoved into her unlaced sneakers and hurried across the grass to catch up with him. They walked in silence, Bridgette constantly scanning her surroundings. She kept waiting for a twig to snap or a random guffaw of anticipatory laughter to ring out, but none came.

Ten minutes in, they crested a small hill. From here they had a bird's eye view of the entire camp: the archery ring with its hay bales and fresh paper targets ready for tomorrow's practice; the craft tent, where flower crowns and cardboard swords had been made in preparation for Saturday's Renaissance festival; the mess hall, where it was a constant struggle getting the kids to eat their food instead of launch it at the next table.

Over the lake hung a full moon, painting the water below in pearlescent gold. While Axel faced the water, breathing in the fresh woodsy air, Bridgette continued to scan the tree line.

"What are you looking for?" Axel chuckled. Bridgette glared at him then turned away, hiding the blush in her cheeks. When she risked looking at him, he was watching her, his head tilted ever so slightly. His brows were raised in anticipation, exposing the pine-green of his eyes.

It was like he was challenging her, almost; certain she wouldn't be honest about the thoughts pogoing around. But maybe if she called him out, foiled his diabolical plan before he could execute it, he'd call the whole thing off and she could go back to her cabin embarrassed but not traumatized. "I'm waiting for your friends to jump out dressed as farmers and chase me around camp, trying to get me to squeal like a pig," she admitted.

Axel's face went through a range of emotions before he settled on confused amusement. "Why...is that a thing you'd be expecting..." he hedged.

Shrugging, Bridgette said, "Why else would you invite me to come out here with you?"

"Because I wanted to? We're friends, aren't we?" Bridgette wasn't sure how to answer this. Sure, he had walked up to her that first day of camp and introduced himself. And yes, he said hi whenever he saw her. They'd even had a couple of conversations that didn't involve camper's allergies or asking the other for bug spray. But he was like that with everyone. He fluttered around camp like a bee, sharing a little bit of himself with each person. They would all flourish because of him.

"Why me, though?" Bridgette asked, ignoring the second half of his statement. She hated how her voice shook and that she even had to *ask* such a question.

As he lowered himself to the ground, his back pressed against the wide base of a tree, Axel asked, "As opposed to who?"

Bridgette followed suit, planting herself in the warm dirt across from him. She tucked her legs as close together as possible to avoid taking up too much of his space. Her gaze remained locked on the tops of her dingy shoes. "As opposed to Marlee, or Leanne, or Anna or Phoebe..." Bridgette thought about listing the other female counselors but she figured Axel got the point. Still, she added, "Literally anyone but me."

"Why them and not you?" Axel asked. Bridgette's fingers become frustrated worms in the topsoil.

"Because they're beautiful," she whispered, looking at him. His eyes were nearly black in the shadows of the oak tree. His head was cocked again, as if he couldn't quite figure her out.

Finally, when she dropped her gaze again, he said, "You're beautiful, too."

Bridgette expected him to laugh, or be wearing some stupid smile that said, *gotcha!* when her attention cut to him. Instead, her heart stuttered at the sincerity on his face.

"I'm chubby," she mumbled around her bottom lip. Her teeth sunk into it as she tried to quell the unease in her stomach. No one had ever called her beautiful. Her friends called her cute and her parents told her she was lovely, but beautiful was not a word with which Bridgette was synonymous.

Axel opened his mouth to say something, then closed it, then opened it again. "And that means you're not beautiful?" he finally replied. The question wasn't spoken softly or kindly, but almost...disappointed. Like he couldn't believe Bridgette would think so low of herself, that chubby and beautiful couldn't go hand-in-hand. Instead of answering, she counted the mosquito bites on her shins. They were drawn to her sweet blood, her mother always said. Made that way by all the snacks she ate, her younger sister always teased.

"Do you know who Josh Groban is?" Axel asked. Bridgette shook her head. "Wow…" He exhaled his disbelief on a small laugh. "That's a problem in itself." He winked, garnering him a half-smile. "He's my grandma's favorite artist. He's mostly a contemporary singer, I guess, sometimes he sings Italian…pop?" Axel made a face, as if he wasn't quite sure that was a real genre. Bridgette laughed, a hiccup of a sound. The grin that crossed Axel's face made Bridgette want to laugh forever.

"Anyway," he continued. "Her favorite song is called 'You're Still You.' It basically says no matter what you go through, no matter how the world tries to shape you, those who love you will always see you. The *real* you." Axel cleared his throat and plucked a dandelion from the earth. He twirled it between his fingers, the flower blurring into a streak so yellow it was as though he were painting with the sun. His voice low, he told Bridgette how his grandma got sick out of nowhere last year, refusing to take treatments because "she'd lived a long, full life." As selfless an act as it was, the pain turned her into someone else. She became short tempered and snippy, angry at the world and everyone in it.

"When the school talent show rolled around this last year, everyone expected me to like…shoot 100 free throws or challenge the football captain to a pushup contest. Instead, I sang that song. It was the last thing my grandma was going to be able to attend, and I wanted to remind her this illness didn't define her. She was still the person who slipped my brother and I money after we mowed her lawn, despite my parents warning her not to. She was still the woman who stayed up making Halloween costumes when we decided last minute to be Power Rangers." Axel nudged Bridgette's shoe with his own. "Don't let others define you, Bridgette Barlow. Don't let society or your friends, or even me, tell you who or what to become. Find the person you want to be and fall in love with her. That way, when someone falls in love with you, because they will, you won't doubt them. That way, when you feel lost, you'll know who to come back to."

It was advice Bridgette often revisited in the years between Orange Lagoon and now. Advice to which she tried to adhere, but failed miserably. She grew to like herself, was able to identify parts to be proud of herself. She knew it was stupid. Beyoncé was right-- she didn't *need* a man to make her feel complete--but there was always something missing in the years she spent without Axel. She didn't *need* him to feel good about herself, but he was always the person who saw her as a whole and loved her despite it all.

On the hill that night, she had wanted to argue. It was her natural reaction to things. Because Bridgette didn't live in kind words or confidence. She tiptoed through life, hoping to avoid bumping into anyone. She wasn't bullied, not really, but she also wasn't noticed.

Sometimes she wondered which was worse...

"Did you win?" she asked Axel when the crickets began to fill the silence.

Chuckling, Axel shook his head. "Absolutely not. But my grandma told me she was proud of me, and that's all I wanted. The rest of it didn't matter."

"Will you sing it for me?" Bridgette asked quietly. She wanted-needed-to hear this song, to catch the words like lightning bugs and feel the warmth of them in her palm. She wanted them to seep into her skin like a sunburn and change her so that she could live up to the expectations Axel had for her.

"Sure," he said without hesitation. He pushed to his feet and offered her his hand. "But only if you dance with me."

Bridgette glanced around nervously, sure that *this* was the moment it would all fall apart. This would be what his friends would catch on camera: the naive moment when she put her guard down and allowed herself to pretend she was a beautiful girl.

"No one is coming, Bridge," he insisted. "It's just you and me. You're safe."

She would hate herself for the rest of her existence if she didn't take his hand, especially if he wasn't playing a joke on her. Before she could register what she was doing, she allowed him to pull her to her feet and tuck her body into his. His hands came around her waist and settled at the small of her back. Bridgette hung her hands on his shoulders, gripping him like a falcon to its prey.

He was already so handsome, the softness of his features had started to melt away, revealing the angles and lines he would be made of six years later when they reconnected at a hotel bar.

She had just finished a four-hour long book-reading and signing. The Michigan weather was at peak fall, the leaves at the top of their game. She had been caught up in watching them sway in the breeze, the grey clouds pregnant with the promise of rain. The bar itself was fairly empty, save for her, the bartender, and a couple of early-evening drinkers. Her plan was to finish her glass of wine then slip up to her room, order a pizza, and call it a night. It was a miracle if she went to bed before midnight most evenings, only pulling herself away from her computer when her back started to curl and her fingers to ache. Her novel, *Marching to Our Own Beat,* was a global hit, gobbled up by youth and adults like fresh-baked cookies. She was grateful for the success, of course, but it was also exhausting.

"Would you sign this for me?" someone asked a second before a well-read copy of her book was slid in front of her. She looked at the cover as if she had never seen it before, and then at the man who had lowered himself onto the stool beside her. It took her brain a second to realign the scattered pieces of her memories. The half-smirk, the pale green eyes, the strawberry blonde waves. Her heart recognized him first. It beat wildly, sensing its other half this close after so many years. Tears filled her eyes immediately but she brushed them away with quick knuckles.

Axel smiled, the gesture crinkling the corners of his eyes. Suddenly, she could hear camp songs screamed by two-hundred kids and smell burnt s'mores melting on pieces of chocolate. "Is it just me," he said, nudging a pen toward her, "or did some of this story feel a bit familiar?"

So much of her summer at Orange Lagoon had shaped the world of Illiana and Roman. Readers had fallen in love with Roman the same way Bridgette had Axel all those summers past.

"What are you doing here?" she whispered.

"Coming to get my book signed."

After she managed to pull her eyes from him and sign his book with a shaky hand, they spent hours catching up on the years that had steamrolled them. Axel taught sixth grade math, which didn't surprise her much. He was always good with kids.

Four drinks later, they confessed they had spent the years pining for one another, both assuming the other had moved on and was living a fulfilled, married life. When they were kicked out of the bar at one in the morning, Axel kissed her all the way to her hotel room and coated her body with a summery sweat until dawn pushed through the curtains.

They tried to make a long-distance relationship work, but Texas to New York pulled them as taut as a bow string, and eventually they snapped with the pressure of missed flights, weekend short visits and late hours. Bridgette was knee-deep in a second book and Axel had been offered a chance to teach math in Spain for a year. A few empty drawers in the other's home and a toothbrush in the holder wasn't enough to keep them together. So on the corner of a busy New York street, they shared one final rain-slicked kiss.

* * *

Three years had passed since that night, yet somehow Axel's hand on her back felt as right as it had when she was a scab-kneed seventeen year old. It was a shame they weren't on that hill again, but instead surrounded by hundreds of his friends and family. And somewhere, his new bride.

"How's my favorite couple?" he asked as they swayed in their little circle. Josh Groban floated around the room, blocking out all other sound except for crickets and his voice in her ear.

Bridgette smiled at him sadly and shook her head. "Not great. I haven't done much writing in about seven months. My agent is not happy," she laughed dryly.

"What happened seven months ago?" Axel asked, his dark brows furrowing slightly.

"I got your wedding invite," Bridgette answered honestly. She remembered the feeling of finality that had ripped through her like she was a piece of anticipated mail. The last ten years had been a merry-go-round of loving and wanting Axel, of taking those feelings and feeding them to Illiana and Roman. She lived vicariously through them, gave them the life she envisioned with Axel. She knew, in the darkest part of her heart, that it would never happen, but hope is a fickle thing that refuses to die until strangled by a Save The Date card.

Axel and Bridgette danced in silence for a few bars of the song, both lost in their own dashed hopes and dreams. He had loved her as much as she had loved him, and letting her officially go had been one of the hardest things he'd ever had to do. They had found themselves in the other--their *true* selves.

"Perhaps," he finally said, "that is the hardest lesson no one tells you you'll learn. That two people can be *too* perfect for each other. Such perfection cannot exist in a world like ours. Maybe one day, but not today."

Bridgette rolled her eyes in jest. She knew those words; she had *written* those words. Or rather, Illiana had scrawled them to Roman in a letter left on his kitchen table. They had found their way back to each other in book two, ten years after their final band camp performance. But they, too, had been unable to work.

Maybe book three would force her to use something more than her life as inspiration.

When the final notes of "You're Still You" faded into a second of nothingness between "The Cha-Cha Slide" kicking in, Bridgette and Axel breathed in each other one last time. She pushed up on her tiptoes and kissed his cheek. "Thank you for that summer," she whispered, squeezing his hand before stepping away.

Outside, the Texas air was dry, but the cool evening breeze took everything down a few degrees. The sky was black marble; the stars grains of salt sprinkled haphazardly along it. Bridgette allowed herself one final moment to love him, to miss him, before she made her way down the rose petal-sprinkled steps.

"Bridge!" Axel's voice rang out. She turned on her heels so quick tiny pebbles kicked up around her. He looked down at her from the top step, the golden light from inside the ballroom illuminating him like the angel he was. Everything she'd become was because of him, because he was too pure and kind and good for her world. He had loved her at her most neurotic, her most stressed, her most defeated. She had what she had because of him. And the things she couldn't allow herself--love, a family--could not exist because he already did.

"Maybe Roman and Illiana can have a happy ending for us," he said, smiling down at her. "Maybe they can stop running from each other and finally..." He shrugged, lost for words. "Finally just be."

Bridgette lifted a sad shoulder. "Maybe," she said.

"Make them get married at the camp," he added, winking. "It feels right."

Nodding once, Bridgette returned his soft, kind smile. "I'll see what I can do," she replied. Axel raised a hand and Bridgette mirrored him. They stood like that, looking at each other for a whole minute, saying goodbye without forcing the words out. Then, because she knew he wouldn't, she turned her back on him.

Three years later...

Bridgette pushed her glasses into her hair and cracked her knuckles. These were the final words she would write for Illiana and Roman, and she needed them to be right. After everything they had gone through, they were finally at their wedding. Members of their former marching bands had come together, learned the music to "You're Still You" for their first dance.

She placed her hand on her swollen stomach and pushed back on the foot pressing against her ribs. "We're almost done, little one," she sighed. Behind her, the door to her office opened. The room was suddenly filled with the woodsy scent she had come to love.

"How's my favorite couple coming along?" her fiancé asked, kissing the top of her head. He set a strawberry smoothie on the only clean spot he could find, then leaned over her shoulder, looking at the screen.

She shooed him away. "Stop. I don't want you to see it until it's done." Nodding her head once, her glasses tipping back onto her nose, Bridgette crafted the final lines of ~~their~~ the story.

For so long, Illiana and Roman had believed their love too perfect to survive in such an ugly, broken world, she wrote. *It would destroy everything, like a rouge ember to a field of dry summer grass. It would burn, and that was why the universe refused them one another. However, as their story faded like sun-exposed book covers, they realized it was losing themselves in the smoke they feared more than anything. Yet somehow, they had managed to blink away the tears and clear their lungs enough to scream for one another. Through the soot they'd tracked each other around the world until they'd collapsed like burning buildings against the other. It had all been worth it, all the burns and the scars, to now stand underneath the setting sun--a fire all its own--and proclaim that they had made it. They had survived. Perhaps* this *was the lesson they had been meant to learn all along: it wasn't supposed to be easy, but it would all be worth it in the end...*

Take Me Home

By Kirsten Stiver

"I'm cold," Gordie Johnson stated weakly.

"The nurse went to get you a warm blanket," his wife, Mina, replied. She leaned over him and stroked his fine, gray hair. He was so thin; so unlike the man she'd been married to for nearly 50 years. She studied his face. His skin was translucent with a hint of jaundice. Gravity drew it down over his features, giving it the appearance of youthfulness, but that fact was denied by the way his eyes sank into their sockets and excess skin sagged loosely around his neck.

"Where's the nurse? I'm cold," Gordie asked, this time a slight irritation in his voice.

"She's coming, Gordie," Mina reassured him.

"So's Christmas," Gordie quipped flatly.

Mina smiled as a tear spontaneously sprung from her left eye and silently rolled down her cheek. He didn't miss a beat. All this pain, all this fighting, and he still made jokes. Sometimes she didn't get it. She got the joke, of course, it was probably the twelve-hundredth time she'd heard it, but the fact that he could still crack a joke with all that was happening, *that* she couldn't always understand. She admired it. She'd even grown to expect it, but understanding it was something Mina had figured would probably never come.

"Sorry it took so long," the young woman apologized as she rushed into the room. She unfolded the blanket and covered Gordie with it. "We were out of blankets on this floor, so I went up to five and got one for you. This one came right out of the dryer!" She announced her accomplishment with pride as she tucked it in around Gordie's feet.

"Mmmmm, thank you," he said softly and sleepily.

"Now get some rest, my love," Mina whispered as she gently squeezed his frail hand. "You'll be up in no time."

Up. *That's right*, Gordie thought. He'd told Mina he would be up and out of bed by June. He had always prided himself on being good for his word. It was imperative that he was good for his word, unlike his father had been – especially when he was drinking. Gordie, now wrapped in a cocoon of warmth, drifted off. *Good for my word. By June*, he thought.

* * *

It was June, 1934, and Gordie was five years old. There was a terrible thunderstorm and his mother, Ivetta Johnson, sat on his bed. His infant sister, Betty, slept soundly in her arms.

"Mama, I'm scared."

"It's just a storm. It'll pass," Ivetta assured her thin, trembling boy.

"Why can't it just rain? Why does there have to be thunder?"

"Now, Gordie, God's just watering the trees and flowers."

"Why does He have to do it so loud? Can't He stop? I don't like it." The rain pounded on the tin roof of the farmhouse. The air smelled damp with a hint of mildew and pine needles.

"The good Lord can make as much noise as He wants to, Gordie. The storm listens to Him, He controls the weather. His voice is like thunder. Or maybe His angels are helping Him water the flowers and that thunder is one of His littlest angels tripping over the watering can," she said with a smile that Gordie couldn't see in the dark, but he could hear in her voice.

Another flash of lightning lit the room as a deafening crack of thunder simultaneously shook it. Gordie leapt into his mother's lap. She shifted Betty to one arm and put the other around Gordie.

"It's alright, *mina älsklingar*," Ivetta reassured her son in her strong Swedish accent. She stroked his soft blonde hair, holding him close, rocking him and his sister. "There will always be rain and there will always be storms, but remember the story of Noah? God put a rainbow in the sky as His promise never to flood the earth again. He is our heavenly Father and He loves us. God *always* keeps His promises."

Ivetta began to sing the hymn, "How Great Thou Art" softly to her son. Gordie drifted off listening to her calming voice; the lyrics painting visions in his mind of stars and mountains and God as a giant superhero whose power controlled the universe. This was a Father he could trust. This was a Father he wanted to make proud. If God always kept His word, Gordie would always keep his promises, too.

* * *

Gordie opened his eyes. He saw a tear rolling slowly down Mina's weary face.

"Don't worry, Mina. *Mina älsklingar*," Gordie whispered.

Mina caught the hint of a smile in the corner of his lips. Her shoulders relaxed ever so slightly. *Here he is, the one in the hospital bed, and he's telling me not to worry.* She closed her eyes, shook her head and sighed. He never ceased to amaze her. He'd been amazing since the day she'd first laid eyes on him.

She and Mary O'Connell had been walking from the dining hall down to the beachfront at Camp Grace. They had just arrived, full of anticipation, and were eagerly exploring the grounds. They'd dropped their luggage off in the girls' cabin, picked their bunks and checked in at the dining hall. They were informed that they had nearly an hour before the counselor's meeting started.

Neither of them had been to camp before. Mary had heard through her church that Camp Grace was in need of summer counselors. Mary was going to college in the fall to become a nurse and had agreed to join the staff to assist the camp nurse.

"Mina, you've just got to come with me! I won't know a soul there. You are great with kids! Why, you're going to be a teacher for heaven's sake! Please say you'll come!"

"But, Mary, my dad really needs help on the farm this summer," Mina had replied, thinking that maybe just this once Mary would listen to reason.

"Mina, they are paying $16 a *week*! That's minimum wage *plus* room and board. Just tell your dad that you'll send all the money home. Besides, they'll have one less mouth to feed while you're gone. Think how much *that* will save them," Mary teased, elbowing her friend in the ribs. Mary knew how much Mina could eat...and still she was as thin as a rail.

Standing a good head taller than most other girls, with thick waves of blonde hair cascading over her strong, farm-chore-chiseled shoulders, Wilhelmina Krause would have easily been super model material...that is if there had been super models in rural Ohio in 1947. However, it was not New York City, and for Mina, being that stately didn't lend any kind of status; it only invited taunting by those she towered over. Enduring years of schoolyard teasing, especially by the boys, Mina was quiet and shy; her clear, sky-blue eyes usually cast downward in the same direction as her spirit.

"Mary, I couldn't..."

"Couldn't say no," Mary interrupted. "I knew it! Hurray! This is going to be so exciting, Mina!"

Mina opened her mouth to protest then closed it again. Once Mary got an idea in her head, there was nothing stopping her. She was just shy of five feet tall, but full of fire as hot as her hair was red. Mary lived for the moment and ran headlong into whatever she pleased with a force so exhilarating it was nearly impossible to fight. Mina knew she was headed to camp; there was no point in resisting. It would be easier to convince her father why she should go than to try to convince Mary she couldn't.

So there they were, making their way past the campfire ring in the middle of the cluster of cabins nestled into the side of a hill a few hundred yards from the dining hall.

"Look, there's the lake!" Mina pointed down the hill. They headed down to investigate. Mary started kicking sand up as soon as they reached the beach. A long, wooden dock jutted out into the clear, sparkling water. A few towels were scattered on the sand while several other teens were splashing and jumping off a raft about 15 yards from the end of the dock.

Then Mina saw him. Gordie Johnson stood on a wooden lifeguard stand looking out over the swimming area. The sun shone on his lightly bronzed skin and a slight breeze ruffled the front of his hair making it look as though he had a horn sticking out of the top of his head. Mina giggled but couldn't take her eyes off him. Mary, who would normally be teasing Mina and trying to play matchmaker already, was surprisingly quiet. Mina looked over to see her staring several yards out into the water. She followed Mary's gaze.

There, on his way toward shore, was the most gorgeous boy either of them had ever seen. He shook the water from his jet-black hair as he strode effortlessly through the waist-deep water. Water droplets glistened like diamonds on his broad shoulders and trickled down his thick, strong arms. Mina had never seen muscles like that, not on a real person anyway. She'd only ever seen such rippling muscles in history books on a statue of Zeus or Poseidon, and thought they could only be sculpted out of stone from some ancient artists' imaginations, not actual human muscle - and certainly not right there in Ohio walking toward them!

Davidh Nephus lifted an arm to smooth back his short, charcoal curls as he strode casually up to the gawking girls and introduced himself. "Hello, ladies, welcome to Camp Grace. Allow me to introduce myself. I am Davidh Nephus, but you can call me Davi." He held out his hand and, for the first time in the history of their friendship, Mina was the first to speak.

"Hello, Davey, I'm Mina, Mina Krause, and this is Mary O'Connell." Mina felt like her voice gave away her jitters, but she was new at this. Mary was always the social bug. However, one glance down at her friend had revealed a star-struck side of Mary she'd never seen before.

"No, *Davi*. It rhymes with Mohave...like the desert," Davi corrected Mina with a smile and a wink. His teeth were perfectly white against his dark, olive skin. It looked like they, too, were chiseled out of marble. Mina shifted her weight back and forth in the awkward silence.

"Oh. Sorry. Davi," Mina corrected herself, her eyes darting down, focusing on her toes.

"It happens all the time," he said with just enough of an accent that he sounded as dreamy as he looked. "It's Greek and not many people have heard it before."

Mina dug her toes deeper in the sand. *What a dunce! I meet a Greek god and I mispronounce his name!* She willed Mary to say something and save her from social suicide. But Mary looked unusually pale. Mina couldn't believe it. *Snap out of it, Mary!* Mina silently begged.

She put her arm around Mary and said, "We're going to be counselors here this summer. Mary's going to assist the nurse and I'm leading crafts."

"I'm teaching archery and survival skills," Davi replied. "And my pal, Gordie, is heading up the waterfront." Davi smiled that smile again and nodded in the direction of the lifeguard stand.

Mina craned her head around and looked up. Her eyes locked with Gordie's. His steel blue eyes instantly calmed her nerves. His mouth slowly widened into a smile, "Hi," he said with a little wave of his hand. The breeze had died down and the hair-horn on his head was gone.

Mina didn't giggle anymore. "Hi," she replied, and gave a little wave back.

"A nurse, are we Miss Mary," Davi commented in more of a statement than a question.

"No. Well...yes. I mean, well...I'm helping the camp nurse here...this summer. But I'm going to Ohio State in the fall to study nursing," Mary stammered, finally finding her voice.

"Gordie here wants to be a doctor; maybe you two could study anatomy together."

Mary's face instantly reddened at Davi's remark. Mina couldn't tell if she was angry or embarrassed. Probably both. Davi may have been full of muscle, but he was certainly lacking in manners.

"You'll have to excuse him, ladies," Gordie said as he climbed down from the guard stand. "It appears my first surgery will be wiring his jaw shut." Mina smiled. Davi glared at Gordie. Gordie gave Davi a theatrical fake punch in the jaw. Davi feigned injury then laughed and put Gordie in a choke hold. Mina looked at Mary while the two boys were wrestling around. The color in Mary's cheeks had returned to normal and Mina sensed that her friend had finally regained her composure.

"If you two don't stop horsing around, you'll be late to the counselor's meeting," Mary announced. "Let's go, Mina," she commanded and marched off the beach, nearly stepping on an abandoned sandcastle.

Mina turned to follow. She looked back over her shoulder at Gordie, and gave a little wave. "Bye!"

Eight weeks later...

"I can't believe there is only a week left of camp," Mina remarked. "This summer has simply flown by."

"If I could freeze time, I would stop it so that this moment could last forever," Gordie said squeezing Mina's hand in his. Mina took a deep breath and sighed. The heavy scent of pine mixed with the earthy smell of dirt and decomposing logs as they walked through the woods.

"Isn't it amazing?" Gordie stopped walking and held his hands up. He looked up and turned around in a circle. "Can you believe how great God is? He made every single tree! And every bird, the water, even the breeze that's blowing through your hair," he said, eyes now on Mina. He reached out and gently pushed back a piece of hair that had blown across Mina's face.

It was Saturday evening. That week's campers had gone home after lunch and long, teary farewells. The counselors were "off duty" until the next afternoon when the last group of campers would arrive.

Davi and Mary had been an item all summer, but Davi had flirted a little too much with one of the other counselors at lunch, which meant there had been more bickering than necking between Mary and Davi when the four of them had gone out in the rowboat that afternoon. The tension between Mary and Davi put Mina on edge, so she had welcomed Gordie's suggestion that they go for a walk after dinner.

"Go get 'em, Tiger!" Davi said boisterously as Gordie held the door of the dining hall open for Mina. Mina visibly cringed and felt her cheeks get hot.

"No need to worry about tigers, Davi. They aren't native to Ohio," Gordie replied in a calm but stern voice.

"You're right there, Gor-do, my apologies," Davi shouted after them.

They had walked in silence for a while before Mina had mustered up the nerve to ask, "How can you stand him? He's such a creep and yet, he's your friend?"

"Davi is a real piece of work," Gordie replied, "but we've known each other since we were little. He's stood up for me plenty of times when I was a skinny, scrawny kid that might not have such a good looking nose if it hadn't been for Davi making sure no one punched me in it." Gordie winked and smiled. "Besides, Mina, he is a child of God. He is one of God's creations and God doesn't make junk. I have to remind myself of that when I'd like to punch *him* in the nose! I'm just thankful that God answers me when I pray for humility and self-control."

Mina smiled. Gordie always had an answer for everything, and the answer was somehow always related to God. She admired his steadfast faith. "Maybe you should stop praying for those things. I think He might have put Davi in your life so you'd get a lot of practice!" Mina laughed and squeezed his hand.

"You might be onto something there," Gordie chuckled and put his arm around her. He pulled her close and held his cheek against hers for a long moment. "He just may have put you in my life for the same reason," he whispered softly in her ear.

Mina's pulse raced. She felt warm and tingly all over. She pulled back and looked deeply into his eyes, "You mean I'm here to keep you humble?" Not able to keep a straight face, she burst into laughter, releasing the tension their hormones were creating.

"No, the self-control part, of course," Gordie answered pulling her close again and leaning in to kiss her. For a split second Mina considered turning her head, but then her lips met his and she'd never been so happy in her life as she lost herself in his embrace.

"Hmmm, I think I've changed my mind," Gordie said still holding Mina, his cheek against hers again. "If I could freeze time, *that's* the moment I wish could last forever." He leaned back and smiled that slow, easy grin that crinkled up his eyes. Mina was sure there was no place on earth she'd rather be.

"Me, too. I still can't believe the entire summer is gone and camp will be over next week. Then we'll be going off to college. Will we ever see each other again?"

"Of course we will. We are meant to be together."

"How do you know that?"

"I knew it the day I met you on the beach, Mina."

"What do you mean?"

"Well, first of all, I thought you were the prettiest gal I'd ever seen." Gordie squeezed Mina and inhaled the intoxicating scent of her hair. "Second, when you were holding a conversation and not star-struck by Davi like Mary was – and *all* girls are – I was impressed. I knew you were different."

"Ugh, his looks are *all* he's got."

"But then you introduced yourself and I knew."

"Knew what?"

"I knew you were my darling."

"What?"

"In Swedish."

"What's in Swedish?"

"My darling."

"Your darling?"

"Yes. My mother always used to call my sister and me her darlings. Whenever we were afraid she'd say, 'Don't worry, *mina älsklingar*,' so when you said your name was Mina, I knew you were *my* darling," Gordie explained, squeezing Mina when he said "my" for a little more emphasis and to hold her closer. "You are my darling, aren't you, *mina älsklingar*?"

"Your darling?" Mina whispered, her throat tight with emotion. "Of course I'm your darling." Mina nuzzled her head against his chest.

Gordie held her close for a long time. Mina could feel his heart beating against her cheek. The rhythmic thumping grew louder in her ear. Then he slowly leaned back, gently lifted her chin and looked into her eyes. The sun was setting and the rosy glow reflected warmly in his eyes. "Be my darling forever, Mina. Say you'll marry me."

Mina was silent. Gordie began to sweat.

Tears welled up in Mina's eyes. "Of course! Yes! Yes, I'll marry you, Gordie!" Mina threw her arms around his neck.

* * *

Mina sighed at the memory and gently stroked Gordie's cheek. "You are so sweet telling me not to worry." She pushed the call button. "Your IV looks like it's coming out."

"It really is okay, Mina," Gordie said earnestly.

"Well, the nurse should be here any minute to check it."

"No, I mean it's okay when it's my time. I'll hear His voice. He'll take me home."

"Nonsense, Gordie, you're going to be just fine, you'll see."

"I don't ever want to leave you, but I have joy in my heart knowing that I'll be in God's presence. It's humbling to think about how much He loves us."

An aide walked into the room and turned off the call button. "What do you need?"

"A million dollars," Gordie chided.

"Oh, Gordie," Mina laughed. She turned to the aide, "What he really needs is someone to check his IV. He seems to have almost pulled it out."

The woman in navy blue scrubs inspected his IV. "Looks like I'd better check with the nurse, but I think we may have to put in a new one. We want to be sure he gets all the antibiotics he needs." She scuttled out of the room.

Mina stood and stretched. She walked over to the window. "Oh, Gordie, look at the sunset! You've just got to see it." She reached for the hospital bed control and slowly elevated his head so he could get a better look.

"One of the two best parts of the day," he smiled.

"You always say it reminds you that God loves you."

"He paints us a reason to start and end each day with a smile. Now, why don't you go home and get some rest? I'll be fine here."

"I can sleep right here, darling."

"You've been here for days. Go home and rest."

"This is a very comfy chair."

"Mina..."

"Oh, alright, there's no sense arguing with you. I think you must be feeling better, you're beginning to act like a stubborn Swede." Mina grinned and tousled his hair. "I'll be back first thing in the morning."

"We can watch the sunrise together."

"I can't think of a better way to start the day. Are you sure you'll be alright?"

"Don't worry, *mina älsklingar*, I'll be fine. I'll sleep better knowing you are getting some rest."

"Good night, my love." Mina leaned over and softly kissed Gordie's forehead and lips.

"Good night," he said, squeezing her hand and closing his eyes.

*　*　**

"There, there, don't worry, *mina älsklingar*, everything will be alright." Ivetta helped Gordie up and brushed the dirt from his shirt. He watched his father, Olie Johnson, stumble into the beer tent. "Now, let's go home and I'll make some apple pie. It will be better than any rides or candy apples here at the fair!" She began to sing, "How Great Thou Art."

"Mama, how can you sing about how great God is when bad things happen?" Gordie asked, his voice tight with anger and frustration. He had tried to protect his mother and little sister from his father's drunken wrath – as best as a skinny seven-year-old could – only to be shoved to the ground where he'd heard Papa's huge, rough hand connect with Mama's cheek.

Ivetta heaved a great sigh and brushed a tear from her swollen face. "Gordie," she had explained, "life can overwhelm you with sadness if you let it. But if you focus on what you *do* have instead of what you *don't*, you'll find joy and contentment in any situation. Why, just look at the sunset! Looking at the beautiful way God paints the sky each day is enough to fill my heart with joy. No matter how bleak things seem, God paints a glorious sunrise and sunset. Twice a day He reminds us of how much He loves us." She picked little Betty up and spun her around.

Betty giggled and Gordie studied the sky. God did paint a picture, every day. There was always a sunrise and there was always a sunset - without fail. Something he could look forward to and Someone he could count on.

* * *

Mina woke early the next morning. She dressed quickly, having taken a long, hot, glorious shower when she'd gotten home the night before. She was eager to return to Gordie's side. It was lonely sleeping in their bed all by herself. Although, she did have to admit, she hadn't felt this well-rested in days, maybe even weeks. She considered breakfast then remembered the amazing breakfast they served at the hospital cafeteria. *I can get there to watch the sunrise with Gordie then, after the doctors do their rounds, I can get scrambled eggs, hash browns, bacon and maybe even an apple fritter. And no dishes to wash!*

Pleased with her plan, she slipped into her loafers, pulled on a light jacket, grabbed her keys and purse then headed out the door. The sky was still dark but a sliver of light was appearing on the horizon. Mina pulled out of the driveway, turned right onto Forest Glade and headed toward the highway. She was pleased that traffic was fairly light this early in the morning. *Just a couple more miles to my exit.* Mina eased into the right lane and began to hum a tune, a loving smile turned up the corner of her lips. *I've got his favorite hymn stuck in my head. Just thinking about him makes me feel like a kid again.* She was just about to pass the last exit before hers when a black Nissan came racing up on her left and cut across her lane to make the off-ramp. Mina slammed on her brakes and swerved to avoid the Nissan, but she caught its rear bumper. The semi-trailer behind her couldn't stop in time. The sound of twisting metal and breaking glass was the last thing Mina heard.

* * *

Gordie awoke with a start. The sun was just beginning to come up over the horizon. There was a smattering of wispy clouds painted pink and purple. *Mina should see this.* He watched as the colors grew brighter until soon the entire sky was the most beautiful rosy pink he'd ever seen. He marveled at the beauty and realized how much better he felt. *Thank you, Lord, for the beautiful picture you paint for me every day. Thank you for every day you give me to see it. Continue to heal me so I can be up and out of here in June like I promised my Mina.*

He looked up as Dr. Cain entered the room.

"Good morning, Gordie," he said, offering his hand. Gordie reached up and shook it.

"What's up, Doc?" Gordie quipped in a weak attempt at a Bugs Bunny impersonation.

"Actually, Gordie, at the rate you are improving, *you* will be the doc that's up soon."

"Really?" Gordie was stunned, then pleased, then upset that Mina wasn't here to hear the good news.

"Yes, your white blood count is nearly in the normal range now. The infection is clearing up. The antibiotics are doing their job. I can't lie to you, Gordie, we were worried about you for a while there, thought your body was too weak to fight the infection after the complications from your surgery. But I'll be the first to admit, miracles still happen."

"That's terrific news! I wish Mina were here to hear this. She'll be so excited!"

"Yes, where is your wife? She's usually camped out right here."

"She looked so exhausted last night, I finally convinced her to go home and get a good night's sleep."

"Good for her. She'll really..."

"Dr. Cain? Can I see you for a minute?" The nurse who'd gotten Gordie a warm blanket the other day came in. She appeared agitated. The two of them stepped out into the hallway.

Must be some emergency. They probably need him in surgery, Gordie thought. He saw Dr. Cain's shoulders slump. They both turned and looked at him. *I know that look. This can't be good. I've had that look when I had to tell a patient bad news. Must be my hemoglobin.*

Dr. Cain nodded to the nurse. She turned and walked back toward the nurse's station. He took a deep breath and headed back into the room.

"Okay, Doc, enough with the 'I have bad news' look. What is it? My hemoglobin?"

"No, Gordie, I'm afraid it's Mina. There's been a car accident. She was killed instantly."

The room began to spin. Gordie tasted bile in the back of his throat. He thought of Mina. How he'd insisted she go home last night. He looked out the window and realized the sunrise had disappeared and the sun shone brilliantly in the bright, blue sky. They would never get to watch the sunrise together again. Silent sobs shook his body.

Doctor Cain put a hand on Gordie's shoulder. "I'm so sorry," he said, then he turned and left the room, closing the door behind him.

* * *

It was June 1st. Mark stood next to Gordie and put his arm around him to steady him. The two looked down at Mina's body in the casket. Everyone else was seated in the sanctuary.

"I should have been here," Mark insisted.

"No, son, there is nothing you or anyone could have done."

"But I could have cut my business trip short. Besides, it doesn't make any sense, you were the one who was in the hospital and now Mom's gone. What kind of a sick God does that?"

"Now, Mark, God's not to blame. The world is full of sin, so we are all dying from the moment we are born. But He sent His son to conquer sin, so because of Jesus' death and resurrection, we have hope. Your mother knew that."

"I know it, too, Dad. My mind knows it, but my heart is still hurt and angry."

"Of course it is. It's okay to have those feelings, Mark. Sometimes I don't know how I'll get through another day, or even the next hour. I miss her terribly."

"Me, too."

The first few notes of "How Great Thou Art" drifted out of the sanctuary. Fresh tears welled up in Gordie's eyes. "It was supposed to be me. I was ready for *me* to go. Not Mina."

"You and Mom always said, 'He is our Creator and, one day, he'll take us all home.'"

"Yes, she's home. He always keeps His promises. But it's in His time, not ours."

"Well, right now I think His timing sucks."

"True." Gordie paused and took a deep breath. "But every day He paints a picture..."

"I know, Dad," Mark said with a sad sigh. "A sunrise and a sunset."

"The two best parts of the day." Gordie looked down and the tears in his eyes spilled down his cheeks. "I will think of you with every sunrise and sunset until He brings me home, too," Gordie whispered as he placed a rose next to Mina. "I love you always, *mina älsklingar*."

Meet the Authors....

Anthony Alaniz is an award-winning journalist, freelance writer, and fiction writer with a career spanning nearly a decade. He lives in southeastern Michigan and currently writes about the automotive industry for several publications while working on several creative projects.

Josh Berry is constantly pushing himself and his creativity by writing pieces that span a wide-range of genres. Josh is also a huge lover of music. While he has been a member of the INK. Writing Group from almost the start, this is his first anthology submission.

Ashley Gilsdorf lives in Michigan with her husband Ben and their three crazy pets. Ashley is a fifth grade elementary school teacher. As a younger writer, Ashley had some writing published through contests. This is Ashley's first published short story. She seeks to explore her passion for writing more deeply, and hopes that this is just a new beginning for her creative voice.

Charlee Kressbach is a retired educator and has written many adventures about Kip, his magical winged horses, the fairies and his large extended family, who he visits regularly. She has published several short stories.

David C. McFarland resides in Adrian, Michigan with his wife, two children, one dog, two cats, two guinea pigs, and two hermit crabs. He would like to thank the pets in helping him overcome his lifelong aversion to squishiness which has also been beneficial to his writing endeavors.

Katey Morgan lives in Michigan with her family. She has been writing since an early age. She also enjoys reading, watching 80's horror movies, and eating cheesecake. This is her first anthology story.

Corinth Panther lives in Michigan with her husband and legion of cats. When she's not working on one of her many writing projects, she can be found seated at a pottery wheel. Corinth is a frequent vendor at the local farmer's market where she sells her pieces; and a yearly attendee at the Lenawee District Library author fair, where she sells her novels.

Lexi Parlier lives in Michigan and has a degree in literature. She has recently published her first novel and loves to spend time with her best friends and her cats: Bruce and Benji. Although her love for pasta is pretty strong, nothing can top her love for books.

Lindsey Sanford is a full-time librarian and a part-time author. She enjoys hanging out with her friends, reading a copious amount, and lazing around when it's storming. Lindsey has been writing since the age of eight, and has recently published her second book, "The New Queen's Crown". She is also the leader of the INK. Writing Group and is constantly amazed by the talent that pours out of it.

Kirsten Stiver is a freelance writer specializing in ghostblogging for various industries. After receiving her technical writing degree from Eastern Michigan University, Kirsten spent several years as a freelance journalist and editor while building a career in sales, advertising and public relations. She switched gears for nearly a decade to be a stay-at-home mom and eventually, caregiver for her mother. When she's not writing, she can be found gardening, scrapbooking, and baking award-winning cheesecakes. Learn more at StiverScript.com.